OLGA

Bernhard Schlink

Translated by Charlotte Collins

WEIDENFELD & NICOLSON

First published in Great Britain in 2020 by Weidenfeld & Nicolson
an imprint of The Orion Publishing Group Ltd
Carmelite House, 50 Victoria Embankment
London EC4Y 0DZ

An Hachette UK company

1 3 5 7 9 10 8 6 4 2

First published in German in 2018 by Diogenes Verlag.

Copyright © 2018 Diogenes Verlag AG Zurich
English translation © Charlotte Collins 2020

The moral rights of Bernhard Schlink and Charlotte Collins to be identified
as the author and translator of this work, respectively, have been asserted
in accordance with the Copyright, Designs and Patents Act of 1988.

A CIP catalogue record for this book
is available from the British Library.

ISBN (Hardback) 978 1 4746 1113 8
ISBN (Export Trade Paperback) 978 1 4746 1114 5
ISBN (eBook) 978 1 4746 1116 9

Typeset by Input Data Services Ltd, Somerset

Printed in Great Britain by Clays Ltd, Elcograf S.p.A.

www.weidenfeldandnicolson.co.uk
www.orionbooks.co.uk

OLGA

Part One

I

'She's no trouble; she just likes to stand and look.'

The neighbour to whom the mother entrusted the child didn't believe it at first, but it was true. The girl, one year old, stood in the kitchen and looked at one thing after another: the table with the four chairs, the dresser, the stove with its pots and ladles, the sink that, with a mirror above it, was also the washbasin, the window, the curtains, finally the lamp hanging from the ceiling. Then she took a few steps, stood in the open doorway of the bedroom and looked at everything in there as well: the bed, the bedside table, the wardrobe, the chest of drawers, the window and curtains, finally the lamp again. She regarded them with interest, although the layout of her neighbour's apartment was no different to that of her parents and the furniture hardly any different, either. When the neighbour thought the small, silent girl had seen all there was to see in the two-room apartment – the toilet was on the landing – she helped her up onto a chair beside the window.

It was a poor part of town, and behind each tall house was a cramped courtyard backing onto another house. The narrow street was packed with all the many people from the many houses, the tram, carts selling potatoes and vegetables and fruit, men and women selling trinkets and cigarettes and matches from hawker's trays, boys selling newspapers, women selling themselves. Men stood on street corners waiting for an opportunity, any opportunity. Every ten minutes a pair of horses pulled a carriage along the tram tracks and the little girl clapped her hands.

As she got older, the girl still liked to stand and look. It wasn't that she had trouble walking; she walked nimbly and confidently. She wanted to observe and understand what was going on around her. Her parents scarcely spoke, to each other or to her. It was thanks to the neighbour that the girl had any words or phrases at all. The neighbour liked to talk, and talked a lot; she'd had a fall, couldn't work, and often helped the girl's mother out. When she took the girl outside, she could only walk slowly and had to keep stopping. But she talked about everything they saw, explained, taught, and expressed her opinion, and the girl couldn't get enough of it; the slow walking and frequent stopping suited her just fine.

The neighbour thought the girl ought to play more with other children. But things could get rough in the dark courtyards and corridors of the building: if you wanted to assert yourself, you had to fight, and if you didn't fight you were bullied. The children's games were preparation in the struggle for survival rather than fun. The girl wasn't fearful or frail. She just didn't like the games.

She learned to read and write before she went to school. At first the neighbour didn't want to teach her, so that when she got to school she wouldn't be bored. But eventually she did, and the girl would read whatever she found at her house: *Grimm's Fairy Tales*, the tales of

Hans Christian Andersen, and Hoffmann's *Shock-Headed Peter*. She would stand and read for hours, leaning on the dresser or windowsill.

The girl would have been bored at school even if she hadn't already been able to read and write. The teacher drummed the letters of the alphabet into the forty school-girls one by one with a cane, and the pronunciation, repetition, dictation and transcription were tedious. But the girl eagerly learned arithmetic so she could check the stallholders when she went shopping, and she liked to sing, and the teacher took the local history class on trips, so the girl came to know the city of Breslau and its surroundings.

2

She came to know that she was growing up in poverty. Just because the school, a new red-brick building with yellow sandstone windowsills and pilasters, was nicer than the other houses in the district, it didn't mean the other houses were run-down. The school was the school. But when the girl saw the stately residences on wide streets, the villas with their gardens, the magnificent public buildings and wide squares and parks, and when she breathed more freely on the riverbanks and bridges, she understood that the poor lived in her neighbourhood and she was one of them.

Her father was a docker, and when there was no work at the docks he sat at home. Her mother was a laundress; she collected laundry from upper-class households, carried it home in a bundle on her head and returned it on her head again, washed and ironed and wrapped in a sheet. She worked day in, day out, but the work didn't bring in much money.

The girl's father had been shifting coal for days on end with no time to sleep or change his clothes when he fell ill. Headache, dizziness, fever – her mother cooled his forehead and calves with a damp cloth. When she saw the red rash on his belly and shoulders, she grew alarmed and fetched the doctor. She too was dizzy and had a fever. The doctor diagnosed typhus and sent them both to hospital. The leave-taking from the girl was brief.

She didn't see her parents again. She wasn't allowed to visit them in hospital in case she got infected. The neighbour took her in and kept telling her that her parents would get better until, after a week, the father died and then, ten days later, the mother. The girl would have liked to stay with the neighbour, and the neighbour would have liked to keep her. But the girl's paternal grandmother decided to take her back to Pomerania.

Things were already not going well between them in the days her grandmother spent arranging the funeral, clearing the house and deregistering the girl from school. The grandmother had disapproved of her son's marriage. She prided herself on her Germanness and had rejected Olga Nowak as a wife for her son, although she spoke fluent German. She had also disapproved of the parents naming the girl after her mother. When she became her guardian, the girl's Slavic name would be exchanged for a German one.

But Olga refused to give up her name. When her grandmother tried to explain the disadvantages of a Slavic name and the merits of a German one, Olga stared at her in incomprehension. When her grandmother presented her with German names, from Edeltraud to Hildegard, that met with her approval, Olga refused to pick one. When her grandmother said that enough was enough and her name was Helga, almost the same as Olga, she crossed her arms, stopped speaking and, when addressed as Helga, did not respond. This continued on the train journey from Breslau to Pomerania and for the first few days after their arrival, until her grandmother gave in. From then on, though, she regarded Olga as a stubborn, ill-mannered, ungrateful girl.

Everything was unfamiliar to Olga. After the big city, the small village and the wide-open countryside; after the girls' school with its different classrooms, the mixed school with boys and girls all in one room; after the lively Silesians, the quiet Pomeranians; after her affectionate neighbour, her unfriendly grandmother; instead of the freedom to read, there was work in the fields and garden. She resigned herself to these things, as poor children do from an early age. But she wanted more than the other children: she wanted to learn more, know more, do more. Her grandmother had no books and no piano. Olga pestered her teacher until he gave her books from his library, and the organist until he explained the organ to her and allowed her to practise on it. When the pastor spoke disparagingly in confirmation class of David Friedrich Strauss's *Life of Jesus*, she persuaded him to lend her the book.

She was lonely. The village children played less than city children: they had to work. When they did play, their games were just as rough, and Olga was skilful enough to hold her own. But she didn't really fit in. She longed for other children who didn't fit in either. Until she found one. He, too, was different. Right from the start.

3

As soon as he could stand he tried to run. One step at a time wasn't fast enough for him, so he would lift his foot before the other had reached the ground, and fall over. He would get up, take one step, then another, feel he was too slow again, try to move one foot before the other had landed, and fall again. Get up, fall down, get up – he kept on, impatient, undaunted. He doesn't want to walk, he wants to run, thought his mother, who was watching, and shook her head.

Even when he learned that his foot should only leave the ground once the other had reached it, he still didn't really walk. He toddled in little scurrying steps, and when his parents put a harness on him and took him out on a lead, as was newly fashionable, it amused them that their little boy pranced like a pony as they strolled along. At the same time, they were a bit embarrassed; the other children walked better in harness.

At the age of three, he ran. He ran all over the rambling house, its three storeys and two attics, down the long corridors, up and down the stairs, through the connecting rooms, over the terrace into the park and down to the fields and the forest. When he started school, he ran to school. It wasn't that he had overslept or lingered over brushing his teeth and would otherwise have arrived late. He just liked to run instead of walk.

At first, the other children ran with him. His father was the richest man in the village; he provided the bread and the wages for many families on his estate, settled disputes, helped maintain the church and the school and made sure the men voted correctly. This made the other children look up to his son and want to copy him, until the respect the teacher showed the boy, and the difference in his manners, language and clothes alienated him from them. Perhaps they would have liked him to be their leader, if he had liked to be one. But he wasn't interested; not because he was snobbish, but because he was wilful. The others should play their own games; he would play his. He didn't need the others. Especially not for running.

When he was seven, his parents gave him a dog. Because they admired everything British and revered Victoria, the widow of the Prussian emperor Frederick III, they chose a Border collie to accompany and protect their son as he ran. This it did, always running ahead, constantly glancing back, with a good instinct for where the boy wanted to go.

They ran on tracks through and around fields, on woodland paths and wide forest aisles, often cutting straight across forest and farmland. The son loved the open fields and the sunlit woods, but when the corn was high he would run right through it to feel the ears on his bare arms and legs, and he would run through the undergrowth so it could scratch and tousle him, and when it clung to him he could tear himself free. When beavers built a dam and dammed up the stream to make a pool, he ran through the pool. Nothing would hold him back, nothing.

He knew what time the train arrived at the station and what time it left. He would run to the station and run alongside the train until the last carriage overtook him. The older he got, the longer he was able to keep up. But that wasn't why he did it. The train took him to the point where his heart couldn't beat or his breath come any faster. He could get there on his own, but it was more enjoyable to be taken there by the train.

He heard the panting of his breath and felt the pounding of his heart. He heard his feet fall on the ground, surely, evenly, lightly, and in every fall there was a rise, and in every rise a hovering. Sometimes he felt as if he were flying.

4

His parents had christened him Herbert because his father had been a soldier with every fibre of his being; he had been awarded the Iron Cross after the Battle of Gravelotte, and wanted his son to be a Herbert, a radiant warrior. He explained to him the meaning of his name, and Herbert was proud of it.

He was proud, too, of Germany, of the young empire and the young emperor, of his father, his mother, his sister, and of the family estate, the impressive property, the stately manor. The only thing that troubled him was the asymmetry of the facade. The main entrance was displaced to the right, with three windows on the left and one on the right beneath five symmetrically positioned windows in the upper floors and roof. No one could explain this proportional imbalance; the house was more than two hundred years old and had only been in the family's possession for a generation.

When Herbert's grandfather had bought the estate from an impoverished aristocrat, he had hoped to be ennobled one day, or, if not him, then Herbert's father, the hero of Gravelotte. The father had also hoped for an aristocratic title to go with the manor and the Iron Cross. But they stayed just plain Schröder. Herbert later hyphenated it with the name of the village. He didn't want to be one Schröder among many.

Despite their dreams of higher things, both grandfather and father were level-headed and hardworking. They made the estate prosperous, built a sugar factory and a brewery, and had enough money to speculate with stocks and shares. The family wanted for nothing, and the children's every wish was fulfilled, as long as that wish was a sensible one: they couldn't skip school and church, but they could go on a trip to Berlin; they couldn't have novels, but they could have patriotic history books; they couldn't have an English model railway with a steam-powered locomotive, but they could have a boat and a gun. After attending elementary school with the village children for four years, Herbert and Viktoria were taught at home: they had a tutor for maths and natural history, and a governess for cultural studies and languages. Herbert learned the violin, Viktoria had piano and singing lessons. Herbert also helped out on the estate so that later on he would know what to expect of the manager and of the farmhands and maidservants.

When it was time for Herbert to go to confirmation class, Viktoria went as well, even though she was a year younger which, strictly speaking, was too young. The parents wanted the siblings to attend confirmation class with the village children, just as they had elementary school, but they didn't want to expose Viktoria to their coarseness without her elder brother to protect her. Not that Viktoria would have been afraid of the other children. Brother and sister both had the arrogant fearlessness of those who will never have to fear or endure suffering. It would do no harm, though, for Viktoria to learn the graces of delicate womanhood, or for Herbert to practise a strong man's chivalry. Both relished their roles. Sometimes Herbert would try to provoke the other children to make rude remarks, so that he could protect Viktoria, but the other children refused to be provoked. They didn't want anything to do with the two of them.

Apart from Olga. Herbert and Viktoria found Olga's interest in their world, her curiosity and admiration, irresistible. The fact that they became friends with her so quickly showed how lonely they had been without knowing it.

5

There is a photograph of the three of them in the garden. Viktoria is sitting on a swing, wearing a puffed dress and a little hat with flowers round the brim; she has opened a parasol, crossed her feet and tilted her head to one side. Leaning on the swing to her left is Herbert, in short trousers and a white shirt; to her right, Olga, in a dark dress with a white collar. These two are looking at each other as if arranging to push the swing together at any moment. All three look solemn and intense. Are they recreating a scene from a book? Are Herbert and Olga indulging Viktoria? Because she's the youngest? Because she knows how to dominate her big brother and older friend? Whatever they're doing, they're doing it with solemn intensity.

The three children look about eighteen, although a note on the back says the picture was taken the day before their confirmation. Both girls are blond; Viktoria's loose curls are spilling out from under the little hat, Olga's straight hair is gathered into a bun at the back of her head. There is a sulky set to Viktoria's mouth which suggests that, when she is not at peace with the world, she can be peevish. Olga has a firm chin, prominent cheekbones and a high, wide forehead, a strong face that becomes more and more pleasing the longer the eye rests upon it. Both look imposing, ready to marry, have children and run a house. They are young women. Herbert is trying to be a young man but he's still a boy, small, sturdy, strong; he is puffing out his chest and holding his head high, but he is no taller than the girls and never will be.

In later photographs, too, Herbert likes to strike a pose, in imitation of the young Kaiser. Viktoria soon grows chubby; eating reconciles her with the world, and the plumpness softens her peevishness while also giving her a childlike, sensual charm. There are no other surviving pictures of Olga for many years; only Herbert's and Viktoria's parents could afford a photographer, and Olga would not have appeared in that one photograph if she hadn't happened to be there at the time.

The year after their confirmation, Viktoria started begging to be sent to the girls' finishing school in Königsberg. At a soirée on a neighbouring estate, the daughter of the house had told her about life at the school as if it were one of luxury and elegance, and as if it were out of the question for any self-respecting girl to grow up among peasants. Her parents didn't want her to go at first, but Viktoria was stubborn. Just as stubbornly, once she had got her way, she continued to insist that the modest life at the finishing school was the epitome of fashionable living.

Olga wanted to go to the state teacher training college for women in Posen. For this, she had to demonstrate knowledge of the final year syllabus at the girls' secondary school. She would gladly have walked the seven kilometres to the girls' secondary school in the district capital every morning and seven kilometres back every evening. But she didn't have money for the school, or an advocate to argue that she should be exempt from paying the fees; the village teacher and pastor both considered further education for girls unnecessary. So she decided to teach herself.

When she went to the girls' secondary school to find out what one needed to know at the end of the final year, she was so intimidated by the large building, the wide staircases, long corridors and multiple doors, the ease with which the girls bustled about the corridor between bells, laughing and chatting, and the confidence of the female teachers entering and leaving the classrooms, heads held high, that she couldn't bring herself to leave the corner by the stairs from which she was watching them. Until one of the teachers, whose classes were over, noticed her. She listened as Olga, close to tears, explained her concerns, then she took her by the arm, led her out of the school and brought her back to her house.

'Religion, German, history, arithmetic, geography and natural history, calligraphy, drawing, singing, needlework – can you manage all that?'

Olga had learned the catechism in confirmation class; she had read Schiller's plays, Freytag's novels and Saegert's *National History of the Prussians*, and she knew poems by Goethe and Mörike, Heine and Fontane, and many songs from Erk's *Garden of German Songs* off by heart. The teacher asked Olga to recite a poem, sing a song and do sums in her head. She inspected the little handbag Olga had crocheted, after which she had no doubts about Olga's skill at needlework, or at drawing and calligraphy. Geography and natural sciences were her weaknesses: Olga knew a lot of trees, flowers and mushrooms, but she had never heard of the evolutionary trees of Carl Linnaeus and Alexander von Humboldt.

The teacher took a liking to Olga. She lent her a text-book on general geography and one on domestic science. If she needed more advice, she could come back. 'And read your Bible – and *Faust!*'

Herbert knew he would join the Foot Guards Regiment when he was eighteen. Before then, he had to pass the high school exams. He obliged his tutor and governess by allowing them to prepare him for it, but his passion was for hunting and shooting, for riding, rowing and running. He knew that one day he was supposed to take over the estate, including the sugar factory and the brewery, and that it was the right thing for his father to introduce him to the business and its management. But he didn't see himself as a lord of the manor and boss of a factory. He saw the great expanse of the landscape and the great expanse of the sky. When he ran, he didn't turn back because he was tired, but because it was dark and he didn't want his mother to worry. He dreamed of running with the sun, all through a never-ending day.

6

After Viktoria left, it took Olga and Herbert a while to establish a new kind of familiarity with just the two of them. Visiting him on his own was different to visiting him and Viktoria. Olga noticed his parents' suspicious glances, and stopped visiting. Herbert hated the knowing smile on the villagers' faces when they encountered him with Olga; he shunned the walks and rowing trips the three of them had taken together so unselfconsciously.

Olga was trying to prepare for the entrance examination, but like the teacher and the pastor, her grandmother didn't think it necessary for her to have any further education, and gave her no peace at home, even when she didn't need her help. So, in summer, Olga fled with her books to an isolated spot at the edge of the forest. This was where Herbert came to visit her. He would bring his dog with him, and sometimes his gun, and he showed Olga a hunting lodge where she could study when it was raining. He often brought a little gift for her: fruit, a piece of cake, a bottle of cider.

When he came, he had usually been running, and would lie down beside her in the grass and wait for her to take a break. Then his first question would be: 'What do you know that you didn't know this morning?'

She liked answering him. In doing so she became aware of what she had retained and what she had forgotten and needed to reread. He was particularly interested in geography and natural sciences and how to live on what the land provided.

'Can you eat lichen?'

'You can eat Icelandic moss. It's a remedy for colds and stomach ache and it can also be used as food.'

'How can you tell if a mushroom is poisonous?'

'You have to memorize them, either the three hundred edible ones or the three hundred inedible ones.'

'What plants grow in the Arctic?'

'Ones that grow in the tundra include—'

'I don't mean the tundra, I mean—'

'The frozen wastes? Nothing grows in the frozen wastes.'

He brought his schoolbooks with him, at her request, and she saw that she had no reason to be ashamed in front of him. The only subject where he was ahead of her was languages; his governess spoke English and French with him, whereas no one spoke with Olga. She didn't need languages for the entrance examination, but she wanted to go to Paris and London one day, cities she had read about in *Meyer's Conversation Lexicon*; she knew her way around them better than Herbert did.

7

Just as Herbert wanted to hear from Olga what she was learning, he wanted to tell her what he was thinking. One day he confided in her that he had become an atheist.

He'd been running again; he stopped in front of her, bent double, hands on knees, and said breathlessly, in a rush: 'There is no God.'

Olga was sitting cross-legged, with a book in her lap. 'One moment.'

He waited until his breath had slowed, lay down beside her in the grass and clasped his hands behind his head, gazed at her, at the dog – she to his right, the dog to his left – and at the deep-blue summer sky with its quick, white scraps of cloud. Then he said it again, quietly and firmly, as if he had made a discovery; or rather, a decision. 'There is no God.'

Olga looked up from her book, and looked at Herbert. 'But?'

'But?'

'What is there instead?'

'Nothing.' Herbert thought her question odd, and

shook his head, laughing. 'There's the world, but there's no heaven and no God.'

Olga set the book aside, stretched out beside Herbert in the grass and looked up at the heavens. She liked the heavens: blue, or grey, and when it was raining or snowing and all you could do was blink into the falling drops or drifting snowflakes. God? Why shouldn't he live in heaven? And come to earth sometimes, in church or nature?

'What would you do if he were suddenly standing in front of you?'

'Like Livingstone in front of Stanley? I'd make a little bow and offer my hand. "God, I presume?"'

Herbert, delighted with his joke, slapped his hands on the ground and laughed. Olga pictured the scene: Herbert in leather knee breeches and a check shirt, God in a white suit and pith helmet, both slightly confused, both consummately polite. She laughed with him. But she felt that you shouldn't make jokes about God. You shouldn't laugh at jokes others made about God, either. Above all, though, she wanted to be left to study in peace. With God, if he wanted to help her, and, if not, then without him.

But Herbert wouldn't leave her in peace. He had identified the ultimate questions. A few days later he asked her, 'Is there such a thing as infinity?'

They were lying side by side again, her face in the shadow of the book she held in her hands, his bathed in sunlight, eyes closed, a grass stalk between his lips.

'Parallel lines intersect at infinity.'

'That's the stupid stuff they teach you in school. If you keep walking on and on between two railway tracks, do you think you'll ever reach the point of intersection?'

'I can only walk a finite distance between railway tracks,

26

not an infinite one. If I could run like you . . .'

Herbert sighed. 'Don't laugh at me. I want to know whether infinity has any meaning for finite people with finite lives. Or are God and infinity the same thing?'

Olga placed the open book on her stomach but didn't let go of it. She would have preferred to hold it up again and continue reading. She had to study. She didn't care about infinity. But when she turned her face to Herbert, he was looking at her in anxious expectation. 'What is it that bothers you about infinity?'

'What bothers me about it?' Herbert sat up. 'If something is infinite, it's also unreachable, isn't it? But is there something that's unreachable per se, not just at the current time and by current means?'

'What do you want with infinity if you reach it?'

Herbert fell silent and gazed into the distance. Olga sat up. What did he see? Beet fields. Green plants and brown furrows in long lines, the lines straight at first, then curving over a dip in the ground towards the horizon and merging finally in an expanse of green. Solitary poplars. A group of beech trees, a dark island in the bright sea of beet fields. The sky was cloudless and the sun at Olga's and Herbert's backs made everything glow, the green of the plants and trees and the brown of the earth. What did he see?

He turned to her and smiled shyly, because he was at a loss, although he was sure there must be an answer to his question, a satisfaction for his longing. She would have liked to put her arm around him and stroke his head, but didn't dare. His longing touched her like the longing of a child for the world. But because he was no longer a child, she sensed in his longing, in his question, in his running, a desperation of which he was not yet aware.

A few days later, he wanted to know if there was such a thing as eternity. 'Are infinity and eternity the same? Infinity relates to space and time, eternity only to time. But do they, in the same way, both transcend what we have?'

'There are people who are still remembered after many years. I don't know about eternally, but Achilles and Hector have been dead for two or three thousand years and we still know about them. Do you want to be famous?'

'I want . . .' He propped himself on his right arm and turned to her. 'I don't know what I want. I want more: more than this, the fields, the estate, the village, more than Königsberg and Berlin and more than the Guards – not because it's the Foot Guards, if it were the Horse Guards it'd be no different. I want something that leaves all this behind. Or beneath – I've read that engineers want to build a machine you can fly with, and I think . . .' He looked over her head and up at the sky. Then he laughed. 'Once you have the machine, and you sit in it and fly in it, that too is just a thing like other things.'

'I'd like to have things. A piano, a Soennecken fountain pen, a new summer dress and a new winter dress, a pair of summer shoes and a pair of winter shoes. Is a room a thing? If that's not a thing, money is a thing, and I'd like to have the money for a room. Perhaps you're . . .'

'Spoiled?' Herbert had turned more towards Olga, propping himself up on the ground with his right hand and tousling his hair with his left. He looked at her.

'I'm sorry. You're not spoiled. You don't know what it's like to be me. But I don't know what it's like to be

28

you, either. I think you have it easier in life than I do. Or I think I would have it easier if I had your life or Viktoria's, and could go to the girls' secondary school and teacher training college just like that. But if I had Viktoria's life, perhaps I'd just want to be sent to finishing school, too.' Olga shook her head.

Herbert waited, but she didn't say anything else. 'I'm going.' He got to his feet, and the dog immediately got to its feet as well and gazed up at him. It had snuggled up against Olga, and she had been stroking it. Olga had grown accustomed to Herbert's unceremonious departures; that the dog could be so close to her one minute and so aloof the next pained her every time.

Herbert set off; the dog jumped up at him, wanting to run with him. Herbert playfully fended him off while at the same time picking up his pace. Then he stopped and turned to Olga. 'I don't have money. I only get money if I need it for something, and then I get as much as it costs. The first time I earn money of my own, I'll buy you a fountain pen.'

He ran off, and Olga gazed after him. Along the edge of the forest, through the beet fields, then onto the path that led to the horizon, where he and the dog got smaller and smaller until they finally disappeared behind the horizon. She gazed after him, full of tenderness.

8

Perhaps Olga and Herbert would not have fallen in love had Viktoria not torn them out of their companionable routine. The finishing school closed for the summer, and when Viktoria came home in July, Olga and Herbert were looking forward to spending the weeks together in the old, familiar way, but they were disappointed. Viktoria wanted something different. She had been invited to balls and parties on neighbouring estates, and expected Herbert to accompany her and do the honours. She had not forgotten Olga, and invited her, out of politeness, to go for a walk and take tea. Afterwards, though, she confessed to her brother that she felt she had nothing in common with this simple girl. 'A teacher? Do you remember Fräulein Pohl, the old spinster we had when the teacher was sick? That's what Olga wants to be? She certainly has as little fashion sense as Fräulein Pohl. I tried to help her, to show her she needs to gather her sleeves and wear her skirts tighter, and she looked at me as if I were speaking Polish. Although actually she probably speaks Polish. Doesn't she have a Slavic face? Isn't Olga Rinke a Slavic name? And why does she act so proudly around me? As if we were equals? She should be happy to learn from me how one ought to dress and behave.'

Herbert was offended by this. Olga wasn't good enough? Her face not beautiful enough? The next time they met, he examined it carefully. He inspected her wide, high forehead, her prominent cheekbones, her green eyes, slightly slanting and wonderfully bright. Could her nose and chin be smaller, or her mouth bigger? But when her mouth laughed or smiled or spoke it was so lively, so dominant, it had to have exactly that nose above it and that chin below. This was even the case when, as now, her lips moved silently as she studied.

Herbert's gaze followed the line of Olga's neck to the nape, paused at the curve of her blouse over her breasts and the suggestion of thighs and calves beneath her skirt, and lingered on her naked ankles and feet. When Olga was studying she took off her shoes and stockings. But although Herbert had often seen her ankles and feet, he had never contemplated them, the dimple beside her ankle bone, the curvature of the heel, the delicacy of the toes, the blue veins. How he would have liked to touch those ankles and feet!

'Why are you staring at me?'

Olga looked at Herbert, and he blushed. 'I'm not staring at you.'

They sat opposite each other, both cross-legged, she with a book, he with a knife and a piece of wood in his hands. He bowed his head. 'I thought I knew your face.' He shook his head and cut a few chips from the wood. 'Now . . .' – he raised his head and looked at her, still blushing – 'now I want to look at it all the time, your face, your neck, your nape, your . . . just you. I've never seen anything so beautiful.'

She also blushed. They gazed at each other, all eyes and soul. They didn't want to look away, to become the familiar Olga and the familiar Herbert again. Until Olga smiled and said, 'What are we going to do? I can't study when you look at me. And when I look at you.'

'We get married, and you stop studying.'

Olga leaned forward and put her arms around his neck. 'You'll never marry me; not now, when you're too young to marry, and not later, because your parents will find you a better match. We have one year until you join the Guards and I go to training college. One year! All we have to do' – she smiled again – 'is agree on when we're going to look at each other and when I'm going to study.'

9

Until autumn, Olga and Herbert could be alone together at the edge of the forest or in the hunting lodge. This was where she studied; this was where he came to find her. But in October it grew cold, and in November the first snow fell. The organist had given Olga the key to the church so she could practise the organ and stand in for him occasionally on Sundays. So she studied in the cold church, which was only heated for services. It was warmer than outdoors, and Olga even found it warmer than at her grandmother's, whose harsh coldness froze her in spite of the warm stove. Olga didn't know that her grandmother found their imminent parting painful, and that this was making her even harsher and colder than usual. Even her grandmother didn't know it.

The church, a neoclassical Romanesque building dating from 1830, had a patron's box, which had passed from the aristocratic former owners of the estate to Herbert's family along with the patronage of the church. Herbert hated his place in the box, where he was exposed to the stares of the congregation every Sunday. This was why it didn't immediately occur to him that the patron's box had its own stove, built in under the floor and lit via the staircase. On very cold days, Olga and Herbert could see their breath in here as well. But the floor was reasonably warm, the roof and balustrade of the box provided some protection against the cold of the nave, the chairs were upholstered, and while she studied Olga knitted a long, thick jersey for Herbert and another for herself. Herbert fantasized about spending winter days in a hunting lodge as cosy as this and shooting the royal stag his father had seen and failed to hit.

He didn't study, although Olga would have liked him to have studied alongside her. Whenever he read anything he soon grew impatient, feeling that the plot could get to the dénouement, the idea to the point more quickly. His tutor had spoken of Nietzsche, the death of God, the *Übermensch*, and eternal recurrence, and Herbert hoped Nietzsche would provide him with answers. Wasn't God also dead for him? Didn't he also wish to surpass himself? Wasn't he also familiar with the recurring cycle of country life? But soon he also found Nietzsche exhausting, and it sufficed for him to pick up one or two turns of phrase and drop them into his conversation. He talked about the two castes, a higher and a lower, without which there could be no culture; about the strength and beauty of pure races, about the fruitfulness of solitude, about the chosen man and the noble man and the *Übermensch* who grows into greatness and at the same time into profundity and awfulness. He decided that he would become an *Übermensch*, that he would not stop or rest, that he would make Germany great and become great with Germany, even if it required him to be cruel to himself and to others. These great words rang hollow to Olga. But Herbert's cheeks were glowing and his eyes shone, and she couldn't help looking at him with love.

They didn't sleep with each other all year. No one would have held it against the son of the lord of the manor if he'd had a dalliance with a village girl, and the villagers would have overlooked any dalliances their daughters had with him. But Herbert wasn't the son of the lord of the manor to Olga, and she wasn't a village girl to him. Nor was their relationship like that of a son and a daughter of the manor, or like two children of a middle-class background. They had found each other in the space between the classes, and didn't feel bound by their conventions. They were alone in the spring and summer at the edge of the forest and in winter in the patron's box; they could have slept with each other, and they decided not to. They took their time.

They kissed and cuddled, they discovered each other, warmed themselves on each other, couldn't take their hands off each other, until Olga extricated herself from their embrace because she wanted to study. If Herbert had not restrained himself, if he came, he would turn away, relieved, spent, resentful, and leap to his feet to run off, or, in winter, to storm off on his skis.

IO

On New Year's Eve the biggest party in the district was held on the Schröder estate. Even neighbours from the old aristocracy came, and Herbert's father wore his Iron Cross and hoped once again for ennoblement. They were celebrating not only the start of the new year, but also the successes of the old: the Civil Code, the initiation of telegraph traffic between Germany and America, the Blue Riband being awarded to the MS *Deutschland*, the raising of the German flag in the new colony of Samoa, and the fact that no Chinese would dare even to look askance at a German ever again. Germany was finally taking its rightful place in the world. At midnight there was a spectacular fireworks display; a pyrotechnician from Königsberg fired off red and white cherry bombs, rockets and fountains against the black sky, and a few blue ones, too, because Britain and France were to be honoured as well. Hadn't the World Exhibition in Paris shown that the young century promised a great future for all the European powers? And Herbert's father had speculated successfully with chemical and electricity shares, and could afford the extravagant fireworks.

Herbert had wanted to invite Olga, but Viktoria had persuaded her parents that Olga's presence would damage her standing with the young people from the old aristocracy. Herbert responded by announcing that he would not attend the party either, and stood firm in the face of Viktoria's tears, his mother's pleas and his father's orders, until Olga persuaded him not to provoke his parents unnecessarily. What if they were to forbid him to meet her?

But the whole village came to the estate for the fireworks, and the people didn't stay on the drive and the court in front of the house; they came around the side of the house to the big terrace where the guests stood looking out over the park, in which the fountain sparkled as it played and the rockets and cherry bombs rose up into the sky. At first the villagers kept their distance from the guests; then, in their enthusiasm at the marvellous illuminations, they pressed further and further forward until they were standing beside and among them. The guests pretended not to notice them, and Herbert's parents pretended not to see Herbert and Olga standing side by side, holding hands and whispering. 'Happy New Year!'

It was a happy new year. Olga passed the entrance exam to the state teacher training college in Posen. She passed with distinction and was awarded a free place in the student hostel. Herbert was proud of Olga, jealous of the importance that studying and knowledge had for her, and discontented when he thought how independent she had become: independent of family, of other people's opinions, of him. She may have been right when she said they could never marry, but he didn't want to accept the reason why, and all he could think was that she didn't need him. Only when he joined the Guards Regiment, after barely managing to pass his exams, was he able to forget his jealousy and malaise and be as proud of himself as he was of Olga.

He sent her a tinted photograph of himself in a blue jacket and white trousers, red collar, red cuffs, the red and blue hat with the little black peak, almost like the caps students wore. He also sent her a photograph of himself in field grey with a golden spiked helmet. She thought he looked good whatever he wore: just tall enough not to be a small man, sturdy and powerful, his angular face cheerful and determined. She loved his eyes: blue and clear, as if free of doubt, but sometimes also with a lost, yearning look that roused her tender feelings.

The photographs arrived accompanied by a fountain pen. It was black, with 'F. Soennecken' engraved on the barrel, which, once the nib was unscrewed, was filled with a pipette. How beautifully it wrote! The upward stroke was thin and the downward stroke thick; even when Olga had corrected something or crossed it out, it still looked good, and she soon stopped making fair copies of her letters to Herbert and simply sent them off. He had bought her the fountain pen, as he had promised, from his first pay packet.

She sent him a photograph, too. She was wearing a wide black skirt and a white tunic with red piping; her neck and her arms were bare. It was reform movement clothing, which Olga had sewn herself. Her hair was in a loose bun, and she wasn't wearing make-up, just a little powder, because her face grew red and blotchy when she was excited. She looked proud – perhaps she was proud, because she was different from the other young girls, and had more than just men and fashion in her head.

II

After two years of training she qualified as a teacher and took up her first position in the autumn – at her old school. Neither the local schools board nor Olga were happy about this, but smallpox had broken out in the village where she was supposed to go, and her old teacher had died suddenly. At least Olga didn't have to live with her grandmother: she moved into the teacher's apartment in the schoolhouse.

She missed Herbert. The school, the church, the houses, the paths, the forest – all were full of memories. Some were of sad occasions: corporal punishment by her grandmother, humiliation by the village children, futile petitions to pastor and teacher to recommend her to the girls' secondary school. Memories of happy times with Herbert and Viktoria had been spoiled by Viktoria's hurtful withdrawal. The hours she and Herbert had spent together on the edge of the forest, at the hunting lodge and in the patron's box remained good memories – and for this very reason, Olga missed Herbert terribly. Since they had parted ways, she to teacher training college, he to the Guards Regiment, they had hardly seen each other.

Occasionally he had passed through Posen on the way home and had waited for her outside the training college; a few times the father of a friend, a fellow student, had invited the two young women on a trip to Berlin and had dropped her off outside Herbert's barracks. Neither of them ever knew when they might manage to be in the same place; their meetings had been impromptu, their embraces hasty, their assurances of love anxious.

In October, Herbert came back to the estate for three weeks. He had volunteered for the colonial force in German South-West Africa, and was on leave until they were due to depart. Olga was teaching; she wanted to do her work especially well in the beginning, to prepare everything, go over everything, and help the pupils as she herself had not been helped. She wanted to find a pupil she could get into the girls' secondary school, one she could give the necessary encouragement and for whom she could secure a free place. But for those three weeks none of this mattered. What mattered was when and where and for how long and how safely she and Herbert could see each other. In the first two weeks they met outside, beneath a mild autumn sun; in the last week they met at Olga's apartment. They made sure they weren't seen when he crept up to her door and she let him in. At the same time, they were too happy really to worry about whether they were talked about in the village.

They had courted and waited for each other for three years; sleeping together now was a fulfilment that those who satisfy their desires immediately simply cannot know. The fear of pregnancy is also something that can scarcely be imagined by those who know how to prevent it. But after such a long separation, Herbert and Olga were so

44

happy to have each other again, not to have to suppress anything any more, not to have to hold anything back, that they didn't waste a moment on fear. For Olga, these weeks were like a dance in which they whirled around each other, then stood quietly, intertwined.

She did not approve of Herbert volunteering for the colonial force. She accepted that soldiers fought, and possibly died, for the fatherland. But Africa wasn't the fatherland. What business did he have there? What had the Herero ever done to him?

But when the ship set off from Hamburg she stood on the Petersen quay, shouted and waved goodbye, joined in the three cheers for the Kaiser and the singing of the national anthem, and heard the steam sirens and whistles of ships big and small sounding the farewell and drowning everything out for minutes on end. Then the noise stopped, silence fell, and when the port and city sounds returned, the ship had vanished from Olga's sight and her hand was clutching the balled-up kerchief she had intended to wave.

12

During Herbert's years in German South-West Africa, Olga was transferred, at Viktoria's instigation. Viktoria didn't think Olga was good enough for Herbert; she wanted to separate the two of them and schemed persistently, with her parents, her friends' parents, the pastor, to achieve this. When Olga realized and tried to speak to Viktoria, Viktoria refused. Through the father of a friend, a senior government official in the provincial administration, she finally succeeded in getting Olga transferred to East Prussia, to the end of the world.

The village lay north of Tilsit. The one road that ran through it was unpaved, dusty when the sun shone, muddy when it rained. In the middle it broadened out into a village green, where the church stood. The houses that lined the road were single-storey and dirty, and the schoolhouse, with the teacher's apartment and garden at the back, was equally shabby.

Olga was in sole charge of all the age groups. The schoolhouse had one room for the small children and one for the bigger ones, and the children were well behaved, and Olga could teach in one room without worrying about discipline in the other. Most of the children lacked any passion for learning, and Olga was satisfied if she could teach them reading and writing and arithmetic, sing 'Now All the Woods Are Sleeping' with them and use it to explain the paths of the sun and moon, the stars, the changing seasons, enjoyment of work and respect for death. Anecdotes about Frederick the Great, 'Old Fritz', were also part of the curriculum, and because Old Fritz had deemed it nonsense that all the woods were sleeping, but that whoever wanted to sing it should do so, she could also use this one song to teach the children about tolerance. Sometimes there was a boy Olga wanted to encourage and send to high school, or a girl she wanted to get into the girls' secondary school in Tilsit, and sometimes she succeeded in overcoming the parents' resistance, persuading the pastor to act as their advocate and gaining a free place for the child.

Poor and wretched as it all was, Olga was glad to be far away from her old village and the old school and away from the scheming Viktoria. She tended to the garden, practised with the church choir she had started on Tuesdays, played the organ in church on Sundays, was active in the union of women teachers, and occasionally travelled to Tilsit to see a concert or performance. She made friends with a family in the neighbouring village and took a particular interest in Eik, the youngest of the many children on their farm.

In the local newspaper she followed intently the colonial force's war against the Herero and the debates about it in the Reichstag. The bourgeois political parties believed in a colonial future for Germany as long as the natives were treated decently and in a Christian manner. The Social

Democrats rejected colonies, believing they were immoral, uneconomical and ruined the character of the people posted there. Attitudes towards the war against the Herero varied accordingly, and the cruelties reported in the press were judged to be either individual misdemeanours or an inevitable characteristic of colonial politics. Olga agreed with the Social Democrats, but she didn't want to imagine an inevitably cruel Herbert and hoped that the nightmare would soon be over.

She wrote long letters to Herbert, and waited for his. When this love that, year in, year out, brought her and Herbert together only for a few hours or days became too hard for her to bear, she thought of the many people for whom separation was the rule and togetherness the exception: soldiers and sailors, explorers, commercial travellers, Poles working in Germany and Germans working in England. Their wives saw no more of their husbands than she of Herbert. She told herself that, in love, two people aren't simply available to one another; they are a gift, and can be a gift to the other in a letter, too. Herbert's letters were often more journalistic, more boastful than she would have liked, but for that very reason they were a gift that made her happy. It was what he was like.

13

Herbert wrote about his voyage to German South-West Africa, about his first encounter with black children who cheerfully dived for the coins he threw for them in the harbour of Monrovia, about the water fight with buckets that the soldiers had on the equator, about their arrival in Swakopmund and the sight of sand, nothing but sand, stretching off into the distance. He had jumped into a dancing boat, been ferried through the breaking waves, and was at last back on dry land; for a long time it refused to keep still beneath his feet, which had grown accustomed to being at sea.

Right from the very first day, Herbert loved the desert. The sand dunes lay to the south, looming up and falling away steeply to the sea, majestic and at the same time, with their soft curves, a picture of sensual beauty. A broad plain of sand and stones extended to the east, grains of sand, some reddish, some greyish, interspersed with dark lichen, pale, thin grass, and occasional little bushy knolls like large mounds of Venus. Herbert loved the concurrence of monotony and diversity, the small variations in stone and sand and vegetation, the winding valleys and hollows and the small, strangely formed mountains that suddenly appeared out of nowhere. And the desert was always vast and empty. Herbert had had no idea that this world of hot sand and burning sun and shimmering air existed. There was no end to its magnificence, even if he rode for days.

When the company reached a train station, where they waited for equipment and supplies, Herbert was delighted by the narrow-gauge railway and rode along for part of the way: painfully slow going up the hill, as fast as an express train on the way down. Sometimes he saw blacks, dark figures in front of their huts, women with short, curly hair and full lips, or fleeting figures that ran away from the company and could not be found by the patrol that set off in pursuit.

One evening, Herbert was sent out on patrol to establish the source of a fiery glow. He saw that the steppe was burning: grass and bushes were aflame, spitting cones of fire beneath dark-red clouds of smoke. Afterwards, he searched for the camp and couldn't find it. When his horse could go no further, he knew he would have to wait for morning and sleep on the steppe. He heard the wail of jackals; it sounded like the howling of dogs or the whimpering of children. They were looking for prey, scented him and drew closer and closer until he was surrounded by their lament, and it overwhelmed him with such dread that his heart almost stopped. He grabbed his gun and sat up and stared into the night, filled with fear of the jackals he could hear, the leopards he knew were there, and the Herero he was fighting. But he saw nothing: no jackals, no leopards, no Herero. All he saw was the darkness of the night, as impenetrable as if a blanket had been spread over him, and he didn't know whether his fear was of what was out there or of something within himself.

But instead of describing his fears to Olga, he tried to impress her. 'Do you know what we're doing for all of you here in German South-West Africa? I read in a newspaper that if we didn't conquer these blacks, it would be a waste to spend any more money on our campaign and the best thing would be to sell the sandpit to Britain. Do you think the same? My response is that the government should not act any differently, unless it wants to betray the mission of all white people and damage our fatherland. We would be losing a paradise!' And Herbert enthused to Olga about the climate, which was better for tuberculosis patients than the climate at home; about the wells that could be dug, the varieties of tobacco, cotton and cactus that could be cultivated, the forests that could be planted, the mines that could be opened, and the factories that could be built. In order to do this, the Germans had to govern. 'With their rebellion, the blacks are trying to seize the government for themselves. They must not be allowed to succeed. We will triumph for their benefit, and for ours. They are people who are still at the lowest level of civilization and lack our highest and best attributes, such as diligence, gratitude, pity, or indeed any ideals at all. Even if they were outwardly to educate themselves, their souls would not keep up. Were they to triumph, it would be a terrible setback for civilization.' He wrote about patrols, skirmishes and pursuits in which he bravely led the way, and about the jubilation when a telegram from the Kaiser praised the officers and troops.

14

It was with particular pride that Herbert recounted the Battle of Waterberg. On 10 August 1904, German troops closed ranks in a loose circle around the Herero camp and behind the mountain. They advanced during the night and attacked on the morning of 11 August.

Herbert's company advanced against the Herero from the south, not up the mountain but over flat terrain. They immediately came under fire. Taking cover behind bushes and in hollows, shooting, jumping up and storming on amid cheers, taking cover again, returning fire again, running further forward, no cheers this time, in leaps and bounds, crouched over, then forming a line with the other soldiers and waiting – these were the first hours of the battle. When the machine guns and artillery arrived, they continued to advance under their protection, until the resistance and counter-attacks by the Herero forced the company to seek cover again behind bushes and in hollows. Whenever it seemed that the Herero would have to yield and flee, the singing and clapping of their women swelled to a crescendo and the Herero would turn the tide, stopping the company's advance or even driving them back. Their aim was to take the Hereros' water source, but they did not succeed that morning or that afternoon. It was only in the evening that they were able to deploy their machine guns and artillery so intensively that the Herero had to abandon it. 'At last the water was ours. Darkness began to fall. Suddenly the tethered balloon the general used for signalling caught fire, broke loose and floated slowly up into the evening sky like a great torch.'

Herbert shot alongside and stormed alongside and fought alongside his comrades, yet he hardly saw a single Herero. He saw his comrades fight and fall. What he saw of the Herero was an occasional head of black hair, or the agile leaps with which they dashed from one hiding place to another. Once he saw a Herero sitting in the crown of a tree get hit, somersault through the air and fall to the ground, and once he saw black bodies and the termite mound behind which they were sheltering get ripped to pieces by a shell and whirled into the air. On every advance he saw fallen Herero, just as on every retreat he saw fallen Germans. But as opponents in the fight, the Herero remained phantoms. 'If only we could have seen the black devils better! Their voices sounded so close. Yet they were so hard to see and get our hands on.'

After taking the water source, the Germans were too weakened to fight on, and the Herero fled eastwards with their cattle. The next day, the Germans took up the pursuit, Herbert among them. Along the road they passed wounded and dying men, elders and children who couldn't keep up and were dying of hunger and thirst, like the cattle crying out their thirst and hunger. Many calves, sheep and goats had their throats cut and the blood sucked out. There wasn't enough water for the fleeing Herero.

There was none for the pursuing Germans, either, who had to turn back.

Herbert never had any real contact with the Herero. During the battle, the machine guns kept them at a distance. After the battle, rifles were enough to keep them at a distance and deny them access to the water sources at the edge of the sandy desert into which they had fled, and where, in the end, they died in their thousands of hunger and thirst.

Then Herbert contracted typhoid fever and was bedbound for a long time. When he recovered, he was put on guard duty before riding out again on patrols, skirmishes and pursuits. When he had time off he hunted guinea fowl, bustards and doves, rock rabbits and genets, springboks and porcupines, gibbons, hyenas, jackals and leopards. He celebrated two Christmases with his fellow soldiers. They cut glittering stars out of tin cans, decorated a camel thorn for their Christmas tree and sang 'Silent Night'. It was a pleasant time.

Sometimes Herbert had to guard captive Herero. He wondered whether they could be forced and trained to work, or whether it was better to replace them with machinery. The closest he had got to them, the closest he had come to empathizing with them, was when he had seen them suffering and dying during the pursuit after the Battle of Waterberg. But they had perished with their cattle, and like cattle; they had been lying on the ground, and he had been on horseback.

15

When Olga saw Herbert again after his return from German South-West Africa, she was so happy that she didn't question him about the atrocities of which she had read. Soon, though, she didn't want to hear any more about battles and skirmishes, patrols and pursuits, either. Nor did she want to hear anything about the endless expanse of the country, the shimmering hot air, mirages and rainbows, the fiery glow and the clouds of smoke from the steppe fires. Nor about what they were going to dig, cultivate and plant, drill and build. 'Those are fantasies! What about now?' She wanted to know whether the blacks were beautiful, the men and the women, how they lived and on what, what they thought of the Germans, what their hopes were for the future. What he had liked over there and what had disgusted him; whether he could imagine living there. What had stayed with him from those two years.

They sat on the bank beside the Neman river. Olga had prepared a picnic, Herbert had rented a carriage, and they had driven for an hour, first from the village to the river and then alongside the river until they found a secluded spot. They spread out a blanket, ate potato salad with meatballs, drank red wine and talked a lot, because they couldn't yet ask the things they wanted to ask: one reads and hears these things – were you with a negress over there? You must have been lonely – have you found someone here? Have your parents found you a wife? What will happen with us, now?

They also talked to chase away the melancholy of the day. It was misty, the sun a blurred disc of light behind a thin cover of cloud, the green of the meadows and the blue of the Neman dulled. It was quiet, no boat chugging past, no gaggling geese, no distant voices. The horse pulled up and chewed the grass; sometimes it snorted, and sometimes the river gurgled.

Olga wasn't satisfied with the information Herbert offered. The women with their broad buttocks weren't attractive to Germans; the Herero lived primitively; they hated the Germans, but knew that the Germans were their fate and their future. What had disgusted him over there: the diseases, typhoid fever and malaria, yellow fever and meningitis; what he had liked – she might not want to hear it any more, but it happened to be true – was that great expanse of land.

'Look at this!' Olga wanted precision now. 'Isn't that an expanse without end? Fields and forests as far as the eye can see. The land's not flat, but the eye passes easily over the gentle hills. Only as far as the horizon, but they have a horizon over there as well.'

'To the left of the hill there's a village; there's another behind the hill, the spire over there is the top of a church tower, and if we travel half an hour downstream we can already see the Queen Luise Bridge. There are people everywhere.'

'Because of the people there's no—'

'Yes, because of the people there's no expanse without end here.'

'What have you got against people? Without them, there's nothing.'

'I don't have anything against people. But they don't have to be everywhere. I can't explain it to you any better.'

Herbert was annoyed, whether by her question or by his inability to explain himself better he didn't know. He felt cornered.

Olga liked it when there was something Herbert couldn't understand, couldn't explain, couldn't express. He was strong, refused to be intimidated and didn't give in, and that was the kind of man she wanted. At the same time, she didn't just want to look up to her man; she liked to have an advantage over him in some ways. But he didn't need to know that, and he certainly didn't need to get annoyed about it.

'When I used to see you running, I always felt you could run on endlessly. That's what you are to me: an expanse without end.' She laid her head on his shoulder. 'Do you still run?'

'Not over there. Here, when I was in Berlin, I used to get up at five o'clock and go running in the Tiergarten. Apart from me, there would just be a few riders around.' He put his arms around her and pulled her down with him so that they lay facing each other, eye to eye. 'In these two years I haven't been with any other woman, white or black. I . . . sometimes when I was alone . . . I wasn't often alone . . . and then I only ever thought of you. I want you. And I'm going to speak to my parents.'

16

He stayed a week. They couldn't live together, either in the village or in the hotel in Tilsit, but it was summer, and the holidays, and there were the fields and the forest. Ours is a field-and-forest love, they laughed.

On the last day, they visited the family Olga had become friends with in the neighbouring village. The farm was small, like all farms north of the Neman; the children were playing between the house and the barns, the rooster was strutting and the chickens scratching, the pigs and piglets running around and the dog and cats lying in the sun. Sanne, the farmer's wife, and Olga greeted each other warmly, and the children were friendly; only Herbert was self-conscious. He had learned to deal with the servants and maids on the estate in an affable, condescending way, but he was unsure of himself with the farmer's wife and children, who were unassuming but not submissive.

Olga tried to draw Herbert into her games with Eik. The little boy was two years old, blond, strong, sturdy, and had as much fun building a tower of wooden blocks with Olga as he did knocking it down. Again and again they built it, and again and again they knocked it down.

Herbert didn't feel like sitting on the ground and joining in; he stood and watched, and pondered Olga's remark, 'This is how I imagine you when you were little!' He couldn't imagine what he had been like when he was little. The only memory he had of his childhood was of the hobby horse he had found in his parents' bedroom before he was given it for his third birthday. Much as he later loved riding, he couldn't run with the hobby horse and so couldn't warm to it. Now he couldn't warm to the impoverished farmyard and the chaos of children and animals and Olga's game with the small, noisy, dirty boy. Luckily the farmer arrived in the evening and listened patiently to Herbert's fantasies about German South-West Africa.

On the ride home in the twilight, Herbert asked what it was she liked about these people, and Olga replied that these were her people, and he shook his head, but didn't ask anything else. They sat beside each other, resentful and silent, until Olga's village came into view. Then she took the reins from his hands, clicked her tongue, drove the horse from a walk to a gallop and steered it onto a path that led across the fields to the forest. Herbert was amazed and enchanted. Olga drove the carriage, jolting and shaking, over the rough terrain; there was a defiant determination in her face, and her hair was blowing in the wind. He didn't know her like this: so beautiful, so strange.

They made love until morning, when he had to go to the hotel in Tilsit and catch the train. She walked home across the fields.

He came back a few weeks later. He had spoken to his parents, and they had threatened to disinherit him if he married Olga. Viktoria had met an officer from an old, impoverished aristocratic family who would marry her, take on the estate and run the business. They had also found a wife for Herbert, an orphan, heiress to a sugar factory; his mother regarded her as someone who would bear him many children, his father as someone who, with Herbert, would turn their sugar factories, hers and his, into a sugar empire. There were arguments and raised voices and tears. In the end, Herbert simply left. An aunt had bequeathed him some money; not a lot, and not enough to marry Olga and start a family. But it would last him a few years. After that it wouldn't be much longer, Herbert knew, before he did something great; he just didn't yet know what it would be.

As with his parents, he neither promised nor refused Olga anything, and Olga didn't press him and didn't complain. It was still summer. The holidays were over, but there was time enough for Olga and Herbert's field-and-forest love. Except that he wasn't fully present. He believed that Olga was full of reproaches that she just wasn't expressing. He was angry with her about it and angry with himself. He didn't want to give in to his parents, and he couldn't break with them. He didn't know what to do. Here too, after a few days, he simply left.

17

He left for Argentina. Another long sea voyage, not with other soldiers this time, but with Germans who wanted to emigrate or who had emigrated and had been back to visit the homeland: the pastor of the German parish in Buenos Aires, businessmen from the Baden Aniline and Soda Factory who planned to travel across the Andes from Argentina to Chile, researchers from a Kaiser Wilhelm Institute following in the footsteps of Alexander von Humboldt, idlers with a penchant for travel and adventure.

Herbert didn't stay in Buenos Aires. He took the boat up the Paraná, a river the like of which he had never seen. He had to admit to himself that the Argentine Paraná might even surpass the German Rhine, and was certainly its equal. Floating forests of orange and willow trees, long, narrow channels that kept seeming to come to an end, then suddenly flowed out into wide, smooth expanses of water, riverbanks devoid of dwellings and full of mysteries, sometimes the screams of monkeys and birds, sometimes profound silence. In Rosario, Herbert took the train to Córdoba, sat in an empty carriage, and, glancing to right and left, looked out over an endless plain. The stations were deserted; the train stopped and carried on, with no voices to be heard. Time and again they passed the corpses of horses and cows lying beside the tracks, and the birds squatting on them, tearing their flesh, didn't even turn their heads. The few trees were stunted and dishevelled; the wind drove cold and keen across the plain and down the train and into Herbert's face until his teeth chattered.

In Córdoba he bought a horse and provisions and set off for Tucumán. Along the way he overtook long processions of wagons with high wheels and round roofs, laden with grain and pulled by six oxen. He encountered herds of wild horses; they stormed up to him at a gallop, accompanied him, dashed off at a gallop again. The villages were small and poor, just a few houses with red facades and white crenellations. The whiteness of endless, dried-out salt lakes dazzled his eyes, and when the wind arose fine red sand penetrated his clothes, his pores, his eyes and ears and mouth. In the evenings Herbert would make a fire and cook whatever he had been able to buy in a village or on a farm: a chicken, meat, potatoes. The weather grew warmer. One day he no longer saw just the same, unchanging plain. A chain of high mountains materialized in the mist on the horizon, bluish with white peaks: the Andes.

He had stopped to rest when he was bitten in the leg by a snake. In the hope of finding a doctor or barber surgeon in the next village he flung himself onto his horse, but soon fell, unable to go on. Hours later — perhaps even days had passed — he came to his senses surrounded by women and children, earth-coloured, with slanting eyes and prominent cheekbones: Indians. There was a cut in his leg where the snake had bitten him, not sewn up but firmly bandaged, not inflamed. Herbert unpicked the seam of his jacket, gave the Indians the gold coins he had hidden there for emergencies, bowed, and rode on. They stared at him intently and followed him with their eyes, slowly turning their heads.

One week later he reached Tucumán. He developed a fever, and by the time he recovered he had run out of time and money and had to turn back without reaching the Andes. In any case, what he loved was the plain, the sky arching from horizon to horizon, the unimpeded view that lost itself in the distance. He would have liked to experience the snows of the Andes.

Instead, he experienced the snows of Karelia. This was his next journey into solitude, immediately after his return from Argentina, on horseback again, this time with a dog. He'd wanted just to spend a few weeks in summer roaming the countryside, experience the white nights, shoot a bear. But he couldn't tear himself away from the gold of the sun that coloured the fog in the morning and the water of the lakes and rivers in the evening and the edges of the sky at night; from the white birch trees and sparse forests; from the swans that rose majestically out of the water, ran across it, launched themselves into the air and landed with equal majesty; from the elk, thickset, powerful, solitary creatures like him. He lived on fish and mushrooms and berries and reconciled himself to the cloud of mosquitoes that accompanied him from morning till night. In September, the colours changed; the birch leaves glowed yellow, the leaves on the bilberry bushes red, the pine trees gleamed green between them and the myriad lichen shone white.

Winter descended earlier than usual. The Karelians had

sensed it and had warned Herbert. He took the view of Bismarck, the Iron Chancellor – we Germans fear God and nothing else in the world – and headed off again. When the first snow fell, Herbert found shelter in a hut. But he couldn't stay; he risked being snowed in and cut off. And so he set out, battled through the snow, and arrived a week later at the post-house where they had warned him, and, in the meantime, assumed that he was lost. They thought he must have given up, in the snow and the cold. But he had not given up. After Karelia, he believed he could do anything. All he had to do was not give up.

18

More journeys followed: to Brazil, the Kola Peninsula, Siberia and the Kamchatka Peninsula. Usually he was away for several months; in Siberia, it was almost a year. Between journeys he visited his parents, who wanted to keep all the options open: Viktoria's marriage to the officer, Herbert's marriage to the heiress. But they lost control of the situation. Viktoria met a young factory owner from the Rhineland who was interested in her but not in the estate; and the heiress was ambitious and independent enough to manage her affairs successfully without Herbert. Herbert hoped that, if the heiress got tired of waiting and Viktoria were married and living in the Rhineland, his parents would transfer the estate to him and Olga after all. But they didn't give up; they pressured and threatened him. Then he would escape his blustering father and weeping mother and go to Berlin, or to Olga.

Sometimes he came for a few days, sometimes for a week or two. He stayed in Tilsit, in a hotel, rented a horse and visited Olga every day. When she was marking exercise books or sewing or cooking or preserving fruit or vegetables, he would sit beside her and watch her. He would tell her about his travels, the journeys he had been on and those he still wanted to make. She listened, and asked questions; she had read about his chosen routes and destinations and was well informed. Sometimes he would rent a carriage and they would go for a picnic beside the Neman; sometimes they would take the first train from Tilsit to the town of Memel, and the last train back, spending the day on the beach at the Curonian Spit.

She would have liked to have him more in her life. She would have liked it if he had sung in the choir with her on Wednesdays, trod the bellows of the organ in the gallery on Sundays, helped organize the Ännchen von Tharau festival in September, and shared her pleasure in watching Eik grow up. But when he accompanied her, he was either too reticent or too forceful with others, didn't find the right tone and didn't feel comfortable.

She saw that the role she played in Herbert's life was like that of a lover in the life of a married man. The married man lives in his own world and goes about his business, and occasionally he sets aside a piece of his life and spends it with his lover, who doesn't share his world and his business. But Herbert was not a married man; there was no wife and no children for him to go back to. Olga knew that he loved her and was as close to her as he was able to be with another human being. He was also as happy with her as he was able to be with another human being. He denied her nothing he was able to give. What she felt she lacked, he wasn't capable of giving.

In May 1910, Herbert gave a lecture to the Tilsit Patriotic Society for Geography and History about

Germany's mission in the Arctic. He happened to have got into conversation with the president of the society at a restaurant, had told him about his travels and a trip he was planning to the Arctic, and had immediately been invited to speak – the president didn't find it easy to get lecturers to come to Tilsit. The garrison school hall was full, and Herbert spoke slowly and tentatively, until the interest he read in his listeners' faces allowed him to present his ideas with increasing enthusiasm.

He recounted Petermann's 1865 attempt to reach the ice-free polar sea which many dreamed of at the time, and of Koldewey's exploration of the east coast of Greenland in 1869–1870 with the two ships *Germania* and *Hansa*, during which the men of the *Germania* obtained important scientific data and those of the *Hansa* spent the winter on a heroic odyssey, drifting on sea ice after losing their ship and making it to a human settlement by boat in the spring. German discipline, German audacity and German heroism had proven themselves splendidly in the Arctic, and were also capable of planting the German flag at the North Pole, which the Americans Cook and Peary falsely boasted that they had conquered. However, German interest had turned away from the Arctic towards the Antarctic – Herbert didn't understand it, nor did he sympathize with the failure of von Drygalski's Antarctic expedition in 1901–1902. 'Germany's future lies in the Arctic. In that land slumbering virginally beneath snow and ice, in the treasures hidden in its earth, in the fishing and hunting grounds, in the North-East Passage connecting Germany quickly and easily with its colonies in the Pacific. The Arctic is not beyond German reach, if we trust in God and ourselves and make the attempt.'

Herbert had been standing behind the lectern; he stepped forward to applause, began to sing the 'Deutschlandlied', and the audience rose to its feet and joined in. '*Deutschland, Deutschland über alles!*'

19

'It's not your sort of thing,' Herbert had said to Olga before the event. But she had come nevertheless, in her best dress, blue velvet with a deep neckline over a thin white blouse with a stand-up collar, and she enjoyed the men's appreciative glances. She waited until the end of the reception, where Herbert was surrounded by admirers and glasses were raised to Germany and the Kaiser and the navy and the Arctic, as well as to him. She was standing by the window, he walked up to her with a radiant face and a light in his eyes, and she told him what he wanted to hear. Wasn't he deserving of praise for this radiance, this light?

They walked to the stables, and despite the lateness of the hour Herbert was able to get a horse and carriage and drive Olga home. He talked and talked. He wanted to hear that she thought that the phrases he was particularly proud of in his lecture were particularly good, that his Antarctic scepticism was justified and his Arctic dreams visionary, and that what he needed to do now was turn his words into action. Until she grew monosyllabic in her assent, and he fell silent.

The moon bathed the fields in white light, and Olga thought of snow and the North and South Poles. But it was May, the air was mild, and a nightingale was singing. Olga put her hand on Herbert's arm; he stopped, and they listened, spellbound.

'They say that the nightingale's song brings the dying a gentle death,' she whispered.

'It sings to lovers.'

'To us.' She nestled against him, and he put his arm around her. 'Why do you want to go there?'

'We Germans—'

'No, not we Germans. Why do you want to go there?'

He said nothing, and she waited. All at once the rush of the wind and the snorting of the horse and the song of the nightingale sounded sad to her. As if they were telling her that her life was waiting, and waiting had no destination, no end. The thought shook her; Herbert sensed it, and answered.

'I could do it. The Pole, the Passage. I haven't been there yet, but I'm convinced I could do it.' He nodded. 'I will do it.'

'Then what? When you've reached the Pole or made the Passage? What will it achieve? You've said yourself that there's nothing at the Pole, and the Passage is blocked most of the time. It'll still be blocked most of the time, even if you make it through once.'

'What are you asking?' He gave her an anguished look. 'You know I don't have answers to your questions.'

'The great expanse? The expanse without end? Is that it?'

'Call it what you like.' He shrugged. 'I have friends in the Guards who say there'll be a war soon. Then I'll go to war. But if there's no war . . . I can't explain it any better.'

You've explained nothing, she thought, nothing.

20

He continued to work on his lecture until the winter. He knew that success in Tilsit did not guarantee success in Berlin, Munich and other capitals and royal seats. There, the audience would be better informed, more critical. There, he would not be able to conceal the fact that Nordenskiöld had already navigated the North-East Passage in 1878–1879, or that the dispute over Cook's claim to have reached the North Pole in 1908 and Peary's that he did so in 1909 demonstrated how difficult it was to prove or refute such a claim. Navigating the North-East Passage would require a great deal of luck and a great deal of time. This was known already; what else was there to know? Reaching the North Pole, and proving it, would be expensive, dangerous and difficult. Flying machines were getting better and better; shouldn't they be the ones to do it, some day?

Herbert's lecture would be on the North-East Passage, the necessity of its German exploration, the necessity of its exploration by him. The Arctic Basin's Siberian coast was poorly charted, worse than that of America and Greenland. Only by exploring and surveying it could a conclusive judgement be made concerning the maritime route between Europe and Asia. Only by closing the ring around the Arctic Basin in this way would it be possible to assess its treasures.

As well as working on the lecture, Herbert wrote letters. He proposed the lecture to scientific societies: geographical societies, ethnological societies, societies for regional geography, for anthropology, for prehistory and marine research. He wrote to von Drygalski requesting a public endorsement; to companies in Berlin and Hamburg requesting donations of equipment, clothing and provisions; to the Brockhaus company suggesting it print postcards with Arctic motifs and use some of the proceeds to support his expedition. When invitations arrived from the various societies, he wrote to local rulers, politicians, industrialists, bankers and other prominent personalities and personally invited them to attend his lecture.

Olga enjoyed Herbert spending a particularly large amount of time with her during the months when he was writing. He would read out to her what he wrote, both the lecture and the letters, and listened to her suggestions. She taught him to write not just a lecture but sections that he could combine as different lectures. She also taught him to speak without notes: first he wrote the sections down and learned them off by heart, later all he needed were notes on the sections. She rehearsed with him, interrupted him, cut him off, asked questions, raised objections. She broke his habit of running his hand across his head when he was confused, and of raising his voice when he was attacked. She turned him into an orator.

She made clear to him that if he wanted to win patrons and champions for his expedition he would have to learn to deal with people of all kinds, and that he could start right here with her, in the village. He did get better at dealing with people. He lost his reticence. But his forcefulness, which sometimes came across as overbearing, remained.

Although Viktoria had now married and moved to the Rhineland, and the sugar factory heiress had found another sugar manufacturer, Herbert's parents continued to insist that Olga was the wrong woman for him. His money – the legacy from his aunt – was running out, and his parents hoped that impending financial hardship would make him compliant. For the time being, though, the only effect was that he stayed in a cheaper hotel in Tilsit, and no longer hired a horse and carriage but took the local train to Schmalleningken and walked, or ran, the six kilometres from the station to the village. Because there was no horse and carriage standing outside the house any more, he could stay the night without attracting attention.

One evening in December, Herbert arrived after dark. Olga was no longer expecting him. Eik was staying with her; the other children on the farm were sick, his mother couldn't keep up with all the wet compresses and rubbing alcohol and linden blossom tea, and she didn't want Eik to get infected. Olga and Eik were playing, and Herbert sat down and joined in, grimacing slightly. The two of them went on playing while Olga cooked, then they all sat around the table and ate, then the two of them played again and Olga washed up. She listened to Herbert and Eik. Ludo was new to both of them; they got annoyed, complained and laughed. After Olga had tucked Eik in – his bed didn't fit in the living room, so had been set up in the kitchen – she turned the lamp above the table right down so that the rest of the room and Eik's bed lay in darkness.

Herbert was reading; the post had brought him Amundsen's report on the navigation of the North-West Passage. Olga had a pile of schoolbooks in front of her. She opened the first, but didn't read it. Tears were running down her cheeks.

'What is it?' Herbert had looked up, got to his feet, and was kneeling beside her. He stroked her hands, whispering: 'What is it?'

'It's just . . .' She too was whispering, but it was enough to open the floodgates to her sobs. 'It's . . .' She shook her head, sobbing.

'What?'

'Can you hear Eik breathing?'

21

On 21 March 1911, Herbert gave his first lecture in Altenburg, and gained his first patron in Duke Ernst von Sachsen-Altenburg.

He wanted to set off on the journey through the North-East Passage in the summer of 1912, and thought a year would be enough to finance and prepare for the expedition. But von Drygalski not only didn't recommend him, he spoke against him, rebuking him for his lack of geographical knowledge and Arctic experience; the Hamburg and Berlin companies were unenthusiastic about providing support; and the Brockhaus publishing house, which initially found the postcard project appealing, lost interest. Herbert had to keep touring his lecture from city to city until the winter of 1912–1913 before he had collected enough to fund the expedition. Only a preliminary expedition, though, on which the equipment and provisions would be tested, the team bonded and trained for life in the Arctic. Herbert hoped the success of the preliminary expedition would trigger a wave of enthusiasm for the main one.

Their destination was Nordaustlandet, an island in

the Spitsbergen archipelago whose little-known interior Herbert wanted to cross before the start of winter. At first, he planned to set off in the early summer of 1913, but then he entered into negotiations to organize a lottery to finance the main expedition, and these became difficult and protracted. By the time he finally left to meet up with the other members of the expedition in Tromsø, it was late July.

On his last evening he said goodbye to Olga. Initially, she had viewed the expedition as one of his many travels, for which she had never seen him on board the train or ship. But then he asked her to meet him in Berlin before they set off, and she came, and didn't know whether to be happy that he needed to be close to her while leaving, or worried that some secret fear was troubling him.

He met her at the train station, took her to the apartment he had rented for the months of preparation for the trip, and left her there alone; he had to go to a meeting and couldn't say when he would be back. He was tense, rushed and jittery, and she didn't want to let this infect her, but as she waited for him in the apartment she grew increasingly uneasy. She paced up and down, from the window in the kitchen, which looked out onto the courtyard, down the corridor and through the drawing room to the window in the study, which looked out onto a square with flowers and a fountain, and back again. She didn't intend to pry, but then she stopped at Herbert's desk after all and went through his papers: bills, lists, prospectuses, cards, excerpts, letters, notes. Among these was a poem in Herbert's handwriting:

First look, consider, then leap, without delay!
Better in the bloom of life to be snatched away
In the struggle to serve humanity – to dare –
Than a hobbled old age, an existence free of care.

Is this what he wanted to tell her? That he was setting off to be snatched away in the bloom of life? Was he not intending to cross Nordaustlandet at all; did he have bigger plans? Was he actually going to attempt the crossing of the North-East Passage, or the conquest of the North Pole? Would he not return before the start of winter?

She found potatoes, eggs and ham in the kitchen and fried them up together for dinner. She found champagne, which she put under running water, and red wine. When Herbert came back, they ate. All he talked about was the ship that he still didn't have and would have to find in Tromsø – what if there were none in Tromsø to be found?

In bed, she said, 'I read your poem.'

He said nothing.

'You're coming back before the start of winter?'

'I wrote that poem years ago. It has nothing more to do with the expedition than with anything else.'

'Before the start of winter?'

'Yes.'

22

In August, Olga read in the Tilsit newspaper that two
members of the team had already left the expedition in
Tromsø and returned to Germany. This could only mean
that Herbert had decided to winter on Nordaustlandet or
Spitsbergen. Olga felt so disappointed, so betrayed, that
she wrote Herbert an angry letter which she sent poste
restante to Tromsø, even though he would only get it
on his return. She had to vent her anger. Two days later
she wasn't angry any more, and wrote another letter with
'Read first!' on the envelope. This too he would only
read on his return: that she was bolstering his spirits in
preparation for the long, dark winter. Now, though, it was
her own spirits she was bolstering. And she reproached
herself. The idea that he could do anything, he just had
to not give up – if only she had tried to talk him out of
his Karelian delusion!

In January she found another report in the Tilsit newspaper. The ship Herbert had purchased in Tromsø was
stuck in pack ice. It had managed to drop Herbert and
three other members of the expedition on Nordaustlandet,
but had not been able to pick them up again. Eventually,

the captain and the remaining team members had left the ice-bound ship and set out to walk the three hundred kilometres to the nearest settlement. The captain had actually reached it, but he was the only one to do so, in a wretched state, with severe frostbite and so exhausted he couldn't speak for days. The others had fallen behind en route.

From then on, the newspaper reported every week on the fate of the expedition. A Norwegian rescue team set off in January, the first German one in February, a second in March, the third in April and the fourth in May. If there was nothing to report about the departure or return of a team, there was still plenty of room for speculation. There were huts in Spitsbergen and on Nordaustlandet, built during previous expeditions, or by whalers and hunters – which might the expedition members have reached? Which route might the team members have taken who set out with the captain but then went a different way? Which route might Herbert and his comrades have taken? Or had they found a hut and built a camp at the start of winter, and would reappear at winter's end in the bay where the ship was supposed to pick them up after their crossing of Nordaustlandet? Experts, real and phoney, piped up with pronouncements that the missing explorers would be found and rescued or that there was no hope for them or that it all depended on how strong the influence of the Gulf Stream was on the climate in Nordaustlandet this winter. There were reports about Herbert, about his experience of war and as a traveller, his energy and determination, but also about his recklessness: the expedition had set out far too late.

Olga read it all, but she wasn't interested in which rescue

team set out when or where. She just wanted to know what had happened to Herbert. In April, two members of the expedition who had set out with the captain but had given up and returned to the ship were rescued; four were dead. The two had had no news of Herbert since he embarked on the crossing of Nordaustlandet in August. In July, a rescue expedition that had focused on the search for Herbert and the routes across Nordaustlandet returned, having found no trace of him. This was now worth only a few column inches in the paper. Austria had just declared war on Serbia.

Olga didn't stop hoping and sending letters to Herbert in Tromsø, poste restante. She knew that the rescue operations had been suspended. But her heart beat a little faster each time the newspaper arrived, until she saw that, once again, there was no report of Herbert's unexpected arrival in a Lapp or Danish settlement. She had read somewhere that a Danish expedition had survived two winters in Greenland. Somewhere . . . she couldn't remember where, and she didn't want to reread it and find that she had misread it and it had only been one winter after all.

She suffered from the fact that Herbert's situation remained strangely unreal. She had been able to picture German South-West Africa soon after he left, because he had described it vividly in his letters and the field post had been reliable and regular. He hadn't written much from Argentina or Karelia, but he had told her a lot about them after his return, as he had after his return from Brazil, Kola, Siberia and Kamchatka. She couldn't picture the Arctic – or was she refusing to do so, out of pique? She was familiar with snow in winter, and had seen drift ice on the Neman and in the Curonian Lagoon. But the snow fields and icebergs and glaciers, the polar bears and walruses, the men swathed in skins and cloth, posing heroically with skis and sledges and dogs – the newspaper illustrator had done drawings from photographs, a few thin black lines that Olga thought looked like caricatures. As if the Arctic were a bad joke. The things she reproached herself with were serious. She had never spoken to Herbert about his projects and plans, never questioned them, never tried to talk him out of them. She had delighted in Herbert's enthusiasm, his radiant face and the light in his eyes, as if he were a child, as if it were all a game. Now the game had cost four lives, or even eight, if Herbert and his comrades did not return.

23

Then Germany declared war on Russia. The Russians occupied Tilsit and had to abandon it again; in between, people stood outside their houses and heard the cannons at Tannenberg. The war moved eastwards, and daily life submitted once again to the laws of farming. In autumn they harvested, threshed and ploughed, in spring they fertilized and harrowed and sowed, and in the wartime summer of 1915 thistles were pulled and weeds hoed and potato beetles picked off just as they were in peacetime summers.

But the men were missing, and some wives and mothers were already wearing black. The old and the young were there, and had to take on what the men would usually have done. Olga's friends in the next village were lucky. The husband was already back from the war; his left arm gone, but he was back. His wife walked through the village with a smile, trying not to flaunt her happiness.

Olga wasn't really hoping any more. Two years had passed since Herbert had set out, and the idea that he would hold out longer than the Danes had done in Greenland was a dream from which Olga awoke as soon as she began to dream it. But his death wasn't real for Olga, either. She thought of Herbert and talked to him, and her connection with him felt no different to the one she had had when she thought about him and talked to him and felt connected to him during all his many travels. She had learned to live with a Herbert who was absent a great deal and for long periods. She didn't have a sense of any break: that now it was too much, now it was too long.

Even if this meant he didn't disappear from her life, the mass slaughter in France finally helped her to grasp the fact of his death. The friend she had made at the women's teacher training college wrote to tell her of the deaths of both her younger brothers and their friends in the great battles on the Marne, in Flanders and Champagne, and for Olga it was as if this generation were being wiped out, and Herbert along with it. She had not been able to picture him in the ice. She could easily imagine him taking part in one of the charges reported in the newspaper, in which young men stormed bravely and cheerfully to their deaths.

That autumn, her grandmother died of consumption. She had complained of abdominal pain and grown thinner and thinner, but hadn't wanted to go and live with Olga and let her take care of her; instead, she had insisted on dying in her own bed. The neighbours, who had looked in on her regularly, found her dead one morning.

When Olga arrived, her grandmother was already lying in her coffin in the church. Olga sat beside her and held the wake. From nightfall till daybreak she sat beside the woman who had taken her in and raised her but not liked her. She did not mourn what had been between her grandmother and herself, which was now over, but that which had never been. She also mourned the unlived lives of those fallen young men, and the life she and Herbert would never have. For the first time, all of it was real: the loss, the farewell, the pain, the mourning. She started weeping and could not stop.

24

She continued to teach in her village until the land north of the Neman, split off from Germany since the Treaty of Versailles and administered by France, was annexed by Lithuania in 1923. After that she taught in a village south of the Neman.

Her great joy in these years was Eik. He was a gifted child, an ingenious and skilful hobby craftsman who built himself a boat and a soapbox cart, and at the same time a dreamer who couldn't hear enough about far-off seas and distant lands. When he discovered Jonathan Swift and Daniel Defoe, Olga told him about Herbert's travels, about German South-West Africa and Argentina and Karelia and the peninsulas and Siberia. She didn't want to tell him about Spitsbergen, or that Herbert was missing, presumed dead.

She presented Eik with a heroic Herbert, not the boy from Pomerania who had overreached himself and frozen to death, but the adventurer full of longing for great expanses and distant lands, who had not given up, who had overcome the worst of hardships and the greatest of dangers. It was as if, although Herbert had failed in the eyes of the whole world, Olga nonetheless wanted to present him to someone as he had seen himself and had wanted to be seen. As if she had forgotten the things she had reproached herself for. Later, she would fear that Eik was taking the wrong path in life, as Herbert had taken the wrong path in life, ultimately taking the path to ruin and becoming the ruin of others. But by then she no longer had any influence over him.

Because he was gifted, he made it out of the village to the city, from the elementary school to the high school and from Tilsit to Berlin. He studied architecture at the Technical University, and sometimes Olga would visit and admire him: tall, blond, with a clear face and blue eyes, athletic, skilled. Later, he won prizes, designed and built a department store in Halle, a hotel in Munich, a consulate in Genoa, and spent many years in Italy. Once she visited him, let him show her around Rome and introduce her to a young woman, a colleague, Jewish, more skilled and, although Eik didn't seem to realize it, cleverer than him. Olga liked the woman, hoped Eik would be able to cope with her superiority, and would have liked to see them get married. At some point, though, she no longer featured in his letters.

In the summer of 1936, Eik returned from Italy and joined the NSDAP and the SS. He fantasized about German *Lebensraum* between the Neman and the Urals, about black earth and grass steppe, rippling wheat fields as far as the eye could see, huge herds of cattle. There were fortified German villages in his fantasy land; apart from these, it was uninhabited. The workers it would need, like oxen before the plough and horses before the cart, would come from somewhere and nowhere in the morning and disappear somewhere and nowhere in the evening. He would oversee, from horseback, the transformation of Slavic poverty into German splendour.

Olga couldn't believe it. She had supported Eik's interests, his reading, his hobbies, had discussed everything with him, encouraged him in everything. And now this? How could he turn his back like this on what she lived and believed? She had never joined the Social Democrats, but she had always voted for them. She had liked the Republic, in which women teachers counted for more than under the Kaiser, could do more and earned more. She had sat on the executive committee of the General German Women Teachers' Association until it pre-empted enforced political conformity by dissolving itself. Right from the start she had rejected National Socialism – once again, Germany was aiming to be too big, after Bismarck had already wanted it and made it too big. And a second world war would follow on from the first.

She tried to talk Eik out of his fantasies. Arable and livestock farming? As a child, hadn't he preferred reading and making things to helping out on the farm? When he was a student, hadn't his geraniums died and his cat run away? Hadn't he studied architecture instead of agriculture? What was this dream of the far horizon and emptiness from sunrise to sunset? There were people living there already, and there was plenty of wheat and cattle in Germany. But she couldn't reach him. He treated her with the affectionate condescension reserved for those who are too old to read the signs of the times.

In the summer holidays Olga caught a fever, thought it was influenza, went to bed, woke up the next morning and could no longer hear. The doctor did this and that;

later, Olga wondered whether he had actually believed in the possibility of recovery or had simply been trying to accustom her slowly to the fact that she was deaf.

She was dismissed, at fifty-three. The schools board wanted to get rid of her anyway. She didn't suit the new age. She wouldn't have stopped teaching if she hadn't had to. But for some time she had assumed that the Nazis would dismiss her, and since then the school had felt increasingly alien to her. And she had been a teacher for more than thirty years – perhaps it was enough.

She moved to Breslau because the school for the deaf there had a good reputation, and thanks to her linguistic skill and vocabulary she became an expert lip-reader. She would have liked to stay in the city after graduating from the school; she had lived long enough in the countryside. But then she moved to a village after all, where life was cheaper. She was a talented and skilful seamstress who had sewn all her own clothes since her time at training college. She found customers in Breslau; some she worked for at their house, while for others she collected the items and brought them back a few days later. The journey took an hour by train.

She resigned herself to her life. She cooked, read, tended her garden, went for walks and sometimes received visits from former pupils, from her friends in the Memel region and their children, from Eik. She missed music every day. She had sung with the children at school, conducted the choir and played the organ at church, and had loved the occasional concerts in Tilsit. She read scores and played the music in her head, but it was a pitiful substitute. She had loved the sounds of nature, too: birds, the sighing of the wind, waves breaking in the sea. She had liked being woken by roosters in summer and by church bells in winter. She was glad she couldn't hear the loudspeakers any more. Under the Nazis the world had become noisy; they had installed loudspeakers everywhere that were constantly pursuing you, blaring out speeches and exhortations and military marches. But nothing is so bad that, in order not to hear it, one would wish to give up hearing the good things as well.

25

The war didn't reach Olga's Silesian village until February 1945. The mayor had reassured them and exhorted them to stay, until one morning he disappeared. Olga couldn't hear the front, but the others could, and she did what the others were doing, packed her bags and left. When soldiers passed by in trucks and tanks she got out of the road, and when low-flying aircraft passed overhead she threw herself into the ditch. The locomotive pulling the train that finally took her was hit by a bomb and exploded.

Amidst all the hurrying and jostling on the road, the clattering and grinding of tank tracks, the howling whistle of low-flying aircraft, the rattling of machine guns, the panic of people fleeing for cover, their screams when they were wounded, the explosion that ripped the locomotive's boiler apart – amidst all this snarling and bellowing of war, Olga was cloaked in utter silence. People's panic was inaudible, their lacerated faces emitted no scream; the tanks silently carved out their path, the planes were soundless shadows flitting over the refugees, and bullets were straight lines of little puffs of dust, until someone was hit and, uncomplaining, acquiescent, sank to the ground or convulsed in the ditch; the explosion of the locomotive was a soundless, brightly coloured ball of fire.

When the locomotive exploded and the train ground to a halt, and she and the others had to continue on foot, it began to snow. At first it snowed softly and was barely visible. Then the snow fell thick and wet and soon lay knee-deep. Every step was an effort, every step was agony. Added to this was the wind: when they were out of the forest, it drove the snow like needles into their faces. When evening came and there was no light, no destination in sight, some gave up. They lay down, a little to the side, under a tree or in a hollow, on their side or back, rucksack under their head, as one would lie down to sleep. Olga had read how people get tired in the snow, sit and lean against a tree to rest for a while, don't feel the cold, and fall asleep, and she had thought it must be a good death. Now she saw them lying there, and whether they were still sleeping or were already dead, it was the same: they were reconciled. They were inviting Olga to lie down with them – with them and with Herbert, who had also died in the snow. But then the thought of Herbert's death made her angry; that stupid death, crossing an island where no one wanted to live, or in a passage no one wanted to use, or heading to the North Pole – whatever Herbert had got into his stupid head. She was so angry that she kept going. No, she didn't want to die like Herbert.

Olga followed the others westwards, on foot, by horse and cart, on trucks, by train. The others would know where to go, she told herself, and if the others were wrong, she didn't know any better. She managed to get across the Elbe before the capitulation, then across the Main, as far as the Neckar. The city was undamaged, and after all the cities with bombed-out, burnt-out, collapsed houses, charred trees lining the streets and in the gardens and parks, ruined wastelands punctuated by chimneys or a church tower or a high-rise bunker, cellars into which people darted like rats, Olga felt she had reached the end of her journey.

The refugee office assigned her a room, and within a few days she was settling in there with her few belongings, and, with joyful amazement, in the city. She was walking down the main street when she passed a photographic studio and went in on a whim. The picture shows a dignified woman with a clear, open face, wrinkles only around the eyes and from the sides of her nose to the corners of her lips, a focused gaze and determined mouth. Her still thick white hair is gathered in a bun, as in the photograph of her as a young girl the day before her confirmation, and she is wearing a black dress with a white collar, not high-necked but with a slightly low neckline. She isn't leaning back or resting on anything; she stands upright, her right hand hanging down and the left held over her bosom in a regal gesture. Nothing, no tension or self-consciousness in her face or bearing, betrays the fact that she is deaf.

She was a quick and meticulous seamstress and soon had enough customers, but no other social contacts, and her life after her flight was even lonelier than before. Her efforts to locate friends from the Memel region through the Red Cross yielded nothing. She took an interest in history and politics, read the paper regularly and attentively, borrowed books and music scores from the public library. She discovered her love of film, and was content to imagine what she couldn't read from the actors' lips.

She sewed for several families until, in the early 1950s, after some back and forth over lost papers and destroyed records, she received the small pension to which she was entitled as a former elementary school teacher in the Prussian school system. After that she only sewed for our family, where she felt particularly welcome: the money she earned with us was sufficient extra income.

Part Two

I

She came every two or three months for several days. She would alter dresses, skirts and blouses, jackets, trousers and shirts, discarded by my aunts and uncles, to fit my older sisters and brother, and, when my brother grew out of them, to fit me. She mended holes that barbed wire or a thorn hedge or a ski pole had ripped, backed fabric, sewed on leather patches. She cut threadbare bed sheets down the middle and sewed them together again along the edges. She also darned stockings and socks if my mother, who didn't really like asking her to do this as it was beneath a seamstress's dignity, couldn't find the time.

When she came, the sewing machine was fetched from my parents' bedroom and set up by the window in the piano and dining room. It was a Pfaff: the name was inlaid in pale wood on the dark wood of the case, it gleamed white against the black of the machine, and was incorporated into the matt-black, cast-iron ornamentation that connected the rods and pedal under the table. For my sisters and brother, the sewing machine was an irritation; it made the room too small and got in the way of their piano, violin and cello practice. I loved it. I thought it was a marvellous device, like the old range in the kitchen with the white enamel front and black hob, the steamroller on freshly tarred streets, the grand black taxis in the nearby square, the black locomotives and green carriages at the station.

And the sound! Clack, clack, clack, clack, clack, clack, a light tapping, soft hissing, gentle slapping, gradually increasing, faster and faster, until it was vibrating as rhythmically and evenly as a swiftly pounding locomotive. Then it would slow down, only to speed up again, or else to die away. When Olga Rinke, whom my mother called Olga and the rest of us called Fräulein Rinke, was there, I played in the dining room. When I'd been made to go to kindergarten I had cried for three days, until my mother had told herself that I would be sufficiently socialized in the big household, with my older siblings, my father, who came home for meals, the guests he often brought back with him, the au pair, and the occasional lodger, and that kindergarten wasn't worth the tears.

Accompanied by the sound of the sewing machine, I would push my train along its tracks, or build houses and factories out of wooden blocks, or play at sewing itself by sitting on my mother's footrest, pushing scraps of cloth over the seat of a stool and tapping my foot on the floor.

For a long time I didn't understand that Fräulein Rinke was deaf. My mother tried more than once to explain to me what being deaf meant. But everything I could do, grown-ups could do, too. So how did it make sense that Fräulein Rinke couldn't hear? My mother covered my ears with my hands, but Fräulein Rinke didn't cover hers.

Sometimes I would yell at her because she didn't answer a question or respond to a request. I didn't dare grab her and shake her, as I would if a member of the family ignored me. But I would get louder and louder, while she carried on doing whatever she was doing until she happened to look up. Then she would say, 'Ferdinand,' with quiet concern, and ask what was the matter, and that would confuse me, and I couldn't remember any more what it was I had asked or requested.

When I was five, I fell ill with a chronic middle ear infection. My ears ached, buzzed, throbbed, oozed, and for days were so blocked that any sounds I heard seemed at best to be coming from a long way off. My mother took me to the ear doctor, who used horrible instruments to pump my nose with air and flush my ears with water, each procedure as bad as the next; while not actually painful, I resisted this aggressive penetration of my head and cried, though my mother had put a sweet into my little red shoulder bag and promised me that I would be allowed to eat it on the way back if I kept still this time. Afterwards, for a while, I could hear – until my ears filled up again and the sounds retreated further and further into the distance.

2

I was often sick, even after the middle ear infections stopped. I kept getting bronchitis, which would confine me to bed for weeks.

I remember the silence in the sick room and muffled sounds in the apartment and outside, snatches of my sister playing the violin or my brother playing the cello. The cries of children playing in the garden, the revving of a truck in the road. I remember the play of light and shadow that the branches of the trees conjured onto the ceiling of my room, and the bright yellow light that swept across my darkened room when cars drove past. And I remember the loneliness I felt when I was ill. I read a lot, and enjoyed it, and my mother came up with all sorts of things to occupy my time, making me learn the old German script and pick old clothes apart to be used to make new ones; and she insisted I keep up with what was being studied in school. But I wanted visitors, company, entertainment.

It wasn't that my mother and sisters and brother didn't take care of me. But my mother was busy with the house-keeping and, as the wife of a pastor, with the women's and girls' groups, and my siblings had school and music lessons and orchestra and choir and sport. They came, sat briefly on the edge of my bed, and went. Sometimes my father even came and sat down, broad and heavy, on my legs, if I didn't pull them out of the way fast enough. He would say a few words, then get lost in thought, especially if it was Saturday afternoon and he had interrupted the preparation of his sermon to come and pay me a visit. My need for entertainment was most reliably satisfied by the women who came and went in our house and who liked to come and sit with me.

There was the cleaning woman who told us repeatedly that ever since knowing people, she had loved animals; but she took me to the church fair, went on the ghost train and chairoplane with me, and read me *Grimm's Fairy Tales* when I was ill, with particular relish for the cruel and gruesome ones. The sexton's wife, who saved her alcoholic husband's job by doing his work for him and came to us to discuss church business, did not have children; she took a liking to me, and lectured me about the curse of alcohol. The female paediatrician we often went to, or who was called to my sickbed, was a mysterious figure: she was the only Jewish woman I knew, and there was an intimacy between her and her receptionist, who had hidden her and saved her during the Third Reich, that I never saw between other women. A friend of my father's, a Russian emigré, often came to stay with us for days and weeks on end, with the nonchalance with which Russians offer and enjoy hospitality, accompanied by his wife and his mentally ill but kind-hearted daughter. As I lay on my sickbed, his wife told me about life in St Petersburg before and during the revolution, and about the exciting journey when Cossacks, hired by her father, brought her from St Petersburg to Odessa and put her on the ship to France. We were often visited by the sister of my father's first wife, who would have liked to inherit and marry my widowed father; she tormented me with cupping glasses and enemas and consoled me with an emotional rendition of a Schumann song, a setting of a Heine ballad about two Napoleonic soldiers.

3

When Fräulein Rinke was there and saw that no one else was keeping me company, she would pick up something to darn and come and sit with me. She told me tales from Silesia and Pomerania, legends of the mountain spirit Rübezahl, and anecdotes about Old Fritz. Like all children, I could listen to the same stories over and over again.

Some anecdotes told of Old Fritz and his flute. I wanted to play as well as he did. His love of the flute was an incentive for me to practise more regularly and for longer; for a while, my flute was my best friend. Old Fritz had taken the flute on one of his late campaigns, but his hands were plagued with gout and he couldn't play; even after he returned to Potsdam and picked up the flute again, he couldn't do it any more. So he had his flutes packed up and put away, saying woefully, 'I have lost my best friend.'

When I was older and read about Robinson Crusoe and Gulliver, travelled with Sven Hedin through the deserts of Asia, and with Roald Amundsen to the South Pole, Fräulein Rinke told me about Herbert's travels and adventures. She left out the war against the Herero: Herbert had travelled to German South-West Africa just as he had felt compelled to go to Argentina and Karelia and Brazil and all those places. She told me about the deserts, the mirages, the brushfires on the steppe, about the snake bite, the swans rising majestically out of the golden water and landing back down on it, about battling through the snow. She didn't talk about Herbert's journey to Spitsbergen and Nordaustlandet. When I asked her what had become of him, she said he hadn't returned from his last journey.

She told vivid stories, and because she always kept her gaze fixed on my face to see if I wanted to ask or say something, I felt she was utterly focused on me. She didn't sit on the edge of the bed; she pulled up a chair alongside and sat upright, with her hands in her lap.

But Fräulein Rinke didn't just tell stories. When she came to my bed and I had a fever, she would cover me with another blanket, or place a cold, wet cloth on my forehead. Her movements were deliberate; she smelled of lavender, her hands were warm and her dignity soothing. I liked her nearness and her touch; as during fittings, when she held up against me the jacket that was to be made shorter or taken in, or, looking for the right place to set the leather patch on the frayed elbow, stroked her hand down my back and arm, and, as she let me go, over my head.

Once – I must have been in the first or second year of high school – my mother asked Fräulein Rinke to come and stay with us for a few days and left me in her care. My sisters were away with the choir; my brother was on a course at the school hostel in the countryside; one of the au pairs who came to us on six-month placements from a school of domestic science had already left and the other hadn't yet arrived; and my mother was accompanying my father on a conference abroad. She spoke English and French, whereas he didn't, and because in those days things weren't interpreted as a matter of course, he needed her. The conference was about the unity of the churches, which was as important to her as it was to him.

Those were silent days. My mother played music whenever she could find the time: piano, a chorale in the morning, Mozart and Beethoven sonatas and Chopin études during the day; my sisters and brother practised their instruments regularly, we played chamber music together, we sang together. After much hesitation, my parents had capitulated to the spirit of the age, purchased a radio, subscribed to a radio magazine, and sometimes put a radio concert on the programme for the family's evening entertainment. There was none of all this in the days with Fräulein Rinke. When I practised the flute, it sounded excessively loud and made me uncomfortable: I stopped practising. I felt it would be unfriendly to turn on the radio, which Fräulein Rinke couldn't hear and couldn't enjoy. We talked to each other, but our talking was not the lively back-and-forth my family usually had at table, rather a concentrated exchange of information. Often, we ate in silence.

I sensed Fräulein Rinke's goodwill. When I got home from school, she would have cooked for me. Meatballs in caper sauce, stuffed cabbage leaves, eggs in mustard sauce, pasta bake. How did she know what I liked? My mother didn't like to spoil us; she wouldn't have asked Fräulein Rinke to cook my favourite dishes. Over the years, Fräulein Rinke must have noticed what I'd particularly enjoyed when we ate lunch together.

In the evenings we sat on the sofa and she told me stories. I would turn towards her, and sometimes she would put her arm around my shoulders and hold me close, and I felt her nearness, her warmth, spoiling me.

4

She had started to tell me about Herbert because I was reading travel and adventure stories, and Herbert had travelled and had adventures. Then she told me stories about Herbert because I had reached the age at which she, Herbert and Viktoria had been playmates. I heard about life on the estate and in the village, the elementary school and the confirmation class, Herbert's dog and his love of running, the games they played together, the walks they went on, the excursions in the rowing boat. She talked about the organ, which the organist had shown her how to play, and about the books the teacher had lent her because she wouldn't give him any peace.

As I got older the conflicts started with my parents, especially my mother. I was reading the wrong books and watching the wrong films, my friends wore blue jeans, smoked and drank alcohol; I wanted to be like them, to fritter the days away with them at the swimming pool and the ice cream parlour. I didn't want to go to church every Sunday any more, either, and I started doing less well at school. I felt my parents ought to understand that I wanted to experiment; they felt I was behaving thoughtlessly and irresponsibly. They weren't particularly strict, but it was the 1950s and, to them, a film with Brigitte Bardot signified vice, a Brecht play communism, and blue jeans were not only unnecessary, as I had plenty of proper trousers to wear, but loutish. When, on top of this, I started to doubt the politics of Adenauer, whom my parents voted for in every election, and wanted to talk to them about it, my father saw this as me attacking the world he had helped to build after the horrors of National Socialism. My mother wanted to reconcile us: he only meant well, she said, and I meant no ill. But we didn't reconcile; we kept having the same arguments over and over again. My older siblings had been smarter; they had avoided confrontation rather than rebel.

Grandparents can sometimes be helpful in a situation like this: more relaxed than the parents, without the responsibility of upbringing, and knowing from experience that conflicts resolve themselves over time and aren't worth making a fuss about. Mine lived a long way away. But when Fräulein Rinke was there, she would interrupt her sewing and listen to me sympathetically. She smiled and shook her head at the smoking, the alcohol and the blue jeans. Although my thoughts about politics must have seemed immature to her, too, she listened to them seriously, not just because she voted for Ollenhauer, not Adenauer, and had joined the union even as a retiree, but because she didn't consider the world of the 1950s as stable and well ordered as my father did; rather, she found it full of uncertainty. She also loved the poems of Brecht almost as much as Heine's.

However, she had no sympathy at all for the fact that I was doing less well at school, and because she had sympathy for everything else, or at least a friendly shrug of the shoulders, I couldn't brush off her disapproval. She told me how she had wanted to go to the girls' secondary school, that she hadn't been allowed to do so, and how she had had to study the syllabus by herself. Learning was a privilege. Not to learn when you were in a position to do so was stupid, spoiled, arrogant. No: the fact that I was doing less well at school was absolutely unacceptable.

5

My mother also worried when I started to become interested in girls. I was not, for the love of God, to fall in love or tie the knot too early. She noted what I was reading: that I was sleeping my way through women's beds with Felix Krull, seducing Madame de Rênal and Mathilde de la Mole with Julien Sorel, and making a harlot of the maid Katyusha with Prince Mitya, and she was appalled.

Fräulein Rinke liked to hear which girl I liked and why, and how I tried to impress her. She told me how she and Herbert had courted each other and eventually come together. Courting takes time, she said. You don't have to be married to sleep together, but you have to have courted and explored each other.

I looked at Fräulein Rinke and tried to imagine her the same age as Emilie, the girl I was in love with. She hadn't worn make-up, she said, as Emilie didn't wear make-up. She had worn simple clothes, as did Emilie. More powerfully built than Emilie, her face flatter, her hair paler – that much I could figure out for myself, but I still couldn't picture her in my mind's eye. It was only later that I saw the photograph of her with Herbert and

Viktoria the day before their confirmation.

I liked that Olga and Herbert had spent a long time courting each other. Emilie was coy, and I had to court her for a long time before she would even let me take her to the cinema. After a year she gave me a first kiss, a quick, light breath on my cheek before she boarded the tram. The next time we met, I put my arm around her after the cinema and she put her head on my shoulder, and we kissed at the bus stop until the tram came. We continued to go to the cinema or a concert or the theatre, but the smooching afterwards was the important bit: in the dark, empty schoolyard, in the park by the church, beside the river. We kissed until our tongues burned.

We kept our love a secret from our families and friends. We wanted to keep it to ourselves. But when Olga told me about the New Year's Eve party Herbert didn't take her to, that she decided to forgo, Emilie's and my secrecy seemed like a betrayal. '*We don't ever want to part, we'll always be together,*' sang Heidi Brühl, and I sang it quietly under my breath as I walked home after my evenings with Emilie. I introduced Emilie to my reluctant parents and my curious siblings, to my friends, and to Fräulein Rinke. When Emilie left me two years later, for a student, they all had words of consolation for me – she was a nice girl, but . . . Everyone had a reason why she hadn't been the right one for me. Only Fräulein Rinke had none. She just said life was a series of losses, and I would learn to make my peace with that in time.

6

In my final years at high school, when I was at home in the afternoon and Fräulein Rinke was sewing, I would make coffee for us and sit with her. She told me about the teacher training college, her first position in Pomerania and her second in the Memel region, the way women teachers were treated under the Kaiser and in the Republic, her involvement with the association of women teachers. She told me about Herbert's travels and the days and weeks they'd spent together.

'We were more patient than you. Back then, people were often separated for months and years, and only briefly together in between. We had to learn to wait. Nowadays you drive and fly and speak on the phone and think the other is available. In love, the other is never available.'

Although Fräulein Rinke looked back calmly on the separations from Herbert, his longing for the great expanse had remained for her a source of annoyance. In the young Herbert she found this longing touching, in the older, absurd. 'The desert – he wanted to dig a well and build factories in the desert of sand, and he wanted to explore the Passage and conquer the Pole in the desert of ice, but it was all far too grand; and anyway, it was all just talk. He didn't want to do anything in the desert, he just wanted to lose himself in it. He wanted to lose himself in the great expanse. But the great expanse is nothingness. He wanted to lose himself in nothingness.'

'Did you ask him why—'

'Oh, child' – this was what she called me – 'we didn't talk about difficult things. When we were together, when we were finally together, he was filled with restlessness. He was always filled with restlessness. He was running inside, and I had to run beside him, and all I could do was breathlessly gasp out things I wanted to say.' She shook her head.

By now, when she talked about Herbert, she no longer left out the fact that he had died on a badly prepared and badly led expedition to the Arctic. Nor did she leave out the war with the Herero any more, and she talked about the First World War, where Herbert would have sought death if he hadn't already found it in the ice, and about the Second. She believed Germany's misery had begun with Bismarck. Ever since he had seated Germany on a horse too big for it to ride, the Germans had wanted everything too grand. Although Bismarck hadn't been interested in colonies, she held him responsible for Herbert's colonial dreams, and for his Arctic nonsense, and for Eik's fantasies about *Lebensraum*, and for the world wars. She thought the reconstruction effort and the economic miracle after the Second World War had got too grand as well.

This was not what I'd learned in my history lessons about the foundation of the German Empire, and I'd never heard anyone say that everything in Germany was getting too grand, either. Nor did I know what to think

126

of the idea that Herbert had wanted to lose himself in nothingness. I knew the feeling that there was nothing for which to strive, nothing for which to work, to believe in or to love that gave true satisfaction. This feeling, transformed into philosophy, was what I understood as nihilism. Herbert's longing for nothingness must, however, have been something else.

7

In the last few years Fräulein Rinke came to us, she still sewed the occasional item now and then, but she would sit at the sewing machine for long periods without working. She would sew a seam and not stop at the end of the material, creating a tangle of threads that she then sat in front of, sad and helpless. She would thread the needle, lean back, put her hands in her lap and turn to look out of the window at the street, where nothing was happening. Or she would fall asleep, and her head would drop onto her chest until the back of her neck hurt and she woke up. 'Your family needs another seamstress.'

But our sewing days were over. My brother was no longer growing out of trousers and jackets and shirts I could wear with slight alterations. My thrifty mother found a second-hand shop with plenty of clothes that fitted me and didn't need Fräulein Rinke's attentions. In any case, my brother and sisters soon left home, and when I finished school I moved out as well.

When Fräulein Rinke started to find sewing tiring, we thought she was just old and tired. But instead she revived;

leaving sewing behind seemed to have set her free. She could do whatever she liked.

After years of living as a lodger, she was allocated her own apartment on the fourth floor of a housing co-op apartment building: two small rooms and a kitchen, bath-room and balcony. The goods yard started right beside the building, and she liked the wide view of the tracks and the old shunting house and the old water tower. In summer she would sit on her balcony, where she cultivated a small garden of flowers in a long window box.

At last she could read everything she'd always wanted to read: classical and modern, novels and poems, books about the history of women, the blind, deaf and dumb, the German Empire and the Weimar Republic, music scores she had played on the organ, and the music she would have liked to play. She went to the cinema and saw films where little was said and a great deal happened: dance films, adventure films, westerns. She continued to vote Social Democrat, attended the trade union demonstration on May Day and church on religious holidays.

Every few weeks my mother would invite her over for Sunday lunch, and I would pick her up and take her home. An uncle had given me an old Opel that the vendor had refused to trade in for a new one. Sometimes I would pick her up on other days, too, and we would do something together: see a film, go sightseeing or to an exhibition, eat at a restaurant. My grandparents, with whom I had spent the happiest holidays of my childhood, whom I'd loved very much and visited often, had died. There was a space in my life.

She was happy for me to accompany her to the art galleries in the nearby town, where she always liked to look at the same pictures. They were paintings from the time when, as a young woman, she had first discovered art, from Anselm Feuerbach and Arnold Böcklin to the impressionists and expressionists. One of her favourite pictures was *The Execution of Emperor Maximilian* by Édouard Manet.

'Why do you love this painting?'

'The emperor is frivolous and absurd, and yet we sympathize with him. The painter is trying to criticize Napoleon's political adventure, but all he can do is romanticize it. And the picture's so huge we could walk into it.'

Sometimes, on our walks, we stumbled over her past. Outside the window of a stationer's shop she recalled her Soennecken fountain pen. 'It was stolen from me when I was fleeing, along with the watch and the ring; not by Russians, by Germans. But I was lucky. Other women had far more taken from them during their flight.' As we were strolling through the market, a man came towards us with a dog, and she stopped and couldn't take her eyes off the dog, a black Border collie with a white neck and blue eyes. 'Herbert's dog looked exactly like that.' She held out her hand, and the dog sniffed it and let her stroke him. Once, when we were on our way home from the cinema and the full moon was particularly large, she thought about her school, and how she had sung 'Now All the Woods Are Sleeping' with the children.

After a day out at the Villa Ludwigshöhe we were sitting on the terrace of its café when she suddenly stopped talking and stared at an elderly lady and gentleman a few tables away; the woman white-haired and plump, the man bald and slim, both well dressed. Olga rose to her feet, took two, three steps towards them, stopped. She just stood there, with her distinctive, upright bearing; then she shook her head and her shoulders drooped. I jumped up, but she waved me away. All she wanted to do was leave.

'What was it?' I waited until we were seated in the car before asking.

She didn't reply until we stopped outside her house. 'The woman was Viktoria . . . that pouting mouth . . . that haughty look. . .' Then she told me how Viktoria had tried to keep her and Herbert apart.

'What happened to her?'

'You just saw her. She's withstood everything, the first war and the second and the bombs and the inflation. She's the kind of person who withstands everything.'

8

Sometimes we drove out to the Forest of Odes or the Hardt Forest and went hiking. Fräulein Rinke had hiking maps and would plan where I should drive and which route we would take.

For me, going for a walk with someone was a chance to talk. Twice a year my father would take us children for a Sunday walk to ask us what we were doing, learning, reading, thinking. My mother, for whom things were real only if they had been the subject of a conversation, and who couldn't talk to her monosyllabic husband anywhere near as much as she would have liked, took advantage of every shopping trip, social call, attendance at church to talk to us children. Hiking with friends was also all about exchanging thoughts and ideas. Fräulein Rinke and I couldn't talk to each other while we were hiking. She had to be facing me in order to understand me, looking at my face, reading my lips.

So we would walk without speaking. Sometimes she would hum under her breath. It took a while for me to get used to it; then I liked it. There was so much to see and hear without the distraction of conversation! Grasses and flowers, the trees' green and multicoloured leaves, beetles, birdsong, the wind in the trees. And there was the smell of freshly felled, resinous wood, and of mouldy wood that had been stacked for a long time, the smell of mushrooms in late summer and rotting leaves in autumn. There was plenty to think about, too, because in our own way Fräulein Rinke and I were in fact in conversation. We would sit on benches not just to rest or have a picnic, but if we wanted to say something, and sometimes there wasn't a single bench we didn't sit on. Fräulein Rinke sat at an angle — side-saddle, as it were; I would sit opposite her, astride, and we would pick up the conversation where it had ended on the previous bench.

If she was tired and didn't want to hike too far, she was happy for me to drive her up the Königstuhl, the mountain behind the city, with its level paths and panoramic view to the west. The view extended over the neighbouring towns on this and the other side of the Rhine, to the smoking chimneys and steaming cooling towers of the Baden Aniline and Soda Factory, to the mountains on the far edge of the plain. In those days there were still a lot of fruit trees on the plain, and the countryside blossomed white and pink in spring. In autumn it was clothed in a bright-leaved blaze of colour; in winter it lay cloaked in white. One evening, fog shrouded the countryside, the towns, the factories, covering the plain all the way from the mountain where we stood to the far mountains, behind which a red sun was setting, gently reddening the fog. It was cold; it must have been a late autumn or early winter evening, and we were freezing, but we couldn't tear ourselves away from the scene until it faded.

9

She was never too tired to walk around the city cemeteries. There were about a dozen of them, and Fräulein Rinke knew them all, but there were some she particularly liked: the Bergfriedhof, the city's largest cemetery, the Ehren-friedhof, the soldiers' cemetery, the Jewish cemetery, and the Bauernfriedhof, the farmers' cemetery outside the city gates. At the Bergfriedhof she liked the variety of paths, tombstones, mausoleums; at the Ehrenfriedhof it was the terrain, which first rose, then fell away, seeming to lead over the field of stone crosses all the way up to heaven; at the Jewish cemetery it was the darkness beneath the old, tall trees; at the Bauernfriedhof it was the red poppies and the cornflowers in the borders of the neighbouring fields. She liked the flowers at the Bergfriedhof, too, but she liked the snow in winter even better, blanketing the paths and graves and lying on the heads and shoulders and wings of the statues of angels and women.

We spoke little, less than on our other walks. Very occasionally Fräulein Rinke would stop, make a comment about a tombstone, or a name or a plant, look at me, and I would reply. Other than this, I heard our steps, the birds, the occasional whirr of a gardening tool or the howl of the machine digging a grave, or the quiet speaking and singing of a funeral party.

I thought I knew why Fräulein Rinke liked walking through cemeteries. Throughout her life she had lost so many people whose graves were unknown or unreachable that she wanted to commune with her dead among the graves of strangers: with Herbert and Eik and her neighbour from the Memel region and her grandmother, and her parents, whom she seldom spoke of but remembered. I understood this. I liked to stand at my grandparents' grave to tell them that I was grateful to them and that I missed them. But when I said this to Fräulein Rinke, she had a different reason.

She wasn't communing with her dead among these strangers' graves. She liked to walk through cemeteries because everyone was equal here: the powerful and the weak, the poor and the rich, the loved and the neglected, those who had been successful and those who had failed. A mausoleum or an angel statue or a big tombstone didn't change any of that. All were equally dead, no one could or wanted to be grand any more, and too grand wasn't even a concept.

'But the Ehrenfriedhof . . .'

'I know what you're going to say. It's too grand, and too much glorification of the soldiers. Everyone should lie together, anyway, the soldiers and the Jews and the farmers and the people buried in the Bergfriedhof.'

They should lie together, she said, and remind us that we are equal in death as in life. Death lost its horror if it were no longer the cruel leveller at the end of a life of inequality, privilege and disadvantage, but simply the continuation of a life in which we were all equal.

I asked her whether souls that had lived in this way migrated through death into a new life. She shrugged. The idea of the migration of the soul was intended to take away people's fear of death, she said. But a person who had understood the truth of equality had no fear of death.

She explained this to me on a bench beneath a big oak tree in the Bauernfriedhof. Then she laughed. 'Here I am talking about equality. You should address me informally, as I do you, and call me Olga.'

10

Talking was more important to her than the things we did together. She could go to an exhibition, take a walk or see a film on her own. Conversing was something she could only do by talking to us, sometimes to my mother and my siblings, but most of all to me.

The talking was never an accompaniment. As on hikes, we didn't speak when we were out together. If we had seen a film, we could only discuss it once we had left the cinema, walked for a bit, found a café and were sitting opposite each other. Being at Olga's was also different to being at home or at friends'. Communal activities like cooking, laying the table, serving the food, clearing away, washing up, which were usually cheerful, chatty and loud, were performed in silence. Olga could have talked. But she didn't like talking without seeing the person opposite her, their reactions, their interjections. Whatever there was to say had to wait until we were sitting opposite each other at the table.

She particularly wanted to talk to me about what was happening in politics and society. She was a daily, attentive, critical newspaper reader.

She followed everything that was published about German South-West Africa very closely. Before long, the thesis was put forward that the Germans had committed genocide against the Herero. Whether because she refused to countenance such an accusation being made against Herbert, or because she had read enough research to the contrary, she reacted fiercely. 'Genocide? Isn't it enough that the Germans waged an ugly colonial war? As others did?' She threw up her hands. 'It has to be something grand – the first genocide!'

When the politics of opening up towards the East began to take shape, she was in favour of it. At the same time, she couldn't reconcile herself to the fact that the land where she had grown up and studied and taught and loved Herbert and cared for Eik was lost. It's not lost, I objected; soon it would be possible to travel there again, perhaps live there again one day. But she just shook her head and said nothing.

She followed the student uprising with sympathy, and soon with scorn. She liked that traditions were being subjected to scrutiny, that the grand talk about culture, freedom and justice was being confronted by social reality, that old Nazis were being unmasked and people were fighting back against house demolitions and fare increases. But she thought us students wanting to create a different kind of human being and a different society and liberate the Third World and stop America's war in Vietnam was too much. 'You and your friends are no better,' she said. 'Instead of solving your problems, you want to save the world. For you too, it's all getting too big, too grand, can't you see that?'

I couldn't see it and contradicted her. 'Too big? Maybe

the task is too big. But not the commitment to it! Colonialism and imperialism are terrible, unjust and immoral.'

'You and your friends are all for morality, I know.' She scowled at me. 'Moralizers want it both ways: big and cosy at the same time. But no one's ever as big as their moralizing, and morality isn't cosy.'

Too big – it was to this that Olga thought she had lost Herbert and Eik, what she held Bismarck responsible for, and what she thought was tempting my generation, too. I contradicted her, accused her of glorifying the small, the trivial, the bourgeois, of not distinguishing between right and wrong, between good big ideas and bad ones. But I didn't convince her.

I I

Since starting to call her Olga, I dared to ask her more direct, personal questions. Her stories about her childhood had accompanied mine, and, as I got older, she told me stories about the rest of her life. But they usually dealt with external events; there was much about Olga's inner life that I didn't learn until I asked her.

I wanted to hear more about her love for Herbert, too. I wanted to know how her love for him was compatible with her rejection of his fantasies, and I learned that love doesn't keep a tally of the other's good and bad qualities.

'Isn't that what determines whether or not they're a good match for you?'

'Oh, child, it's not qualities that make two people a match. It's love that does that.'

Then I wanted to know how long love lasts; how long after death, and what still sustained her mourning for Herbert after fifty years.

'I don't mourn Herbert. I live with him. Perhaps it's because I lost my hearing and didn't get to know many people after that. The people I was close to before, I'm still close to: my grandmother, Eik, my friend in the neighbouring village, a colleague, a few pupils. I talk to them sometimes. There are others who are still present for me, too: the schools inspector, the girls from the teacher training college, Herbert's parents, the pastors in whose churches I played the organ. But I don't talk to them. After Herbert's death, I didn't want anything to do with him for a long time. But when I couldn't hear any more, and he knocked again, I opened the door to him.'

Then I asked her why she hadn't taken another man after Herbert's death.

'Taken? What a thing that would be, if one could take men like apples off a tree. And if good men hung around as abundantly as good apples. Who was I supposed to find in my village? I could have gone to Tilsit and sung in the choral society or joined the committee for the Ännchen von Tharau festival and hoped to find someone. But there were so many who didn't come back from the war, and other women were already courting the few who had returned. If an apple had fallen into my lap . . .' She laughed quietly. Then she nodded. 'That's how it is, child. You can't make the best of what you're given unless you accept it.'

12

After a few semesters I transferred to a different city and a different university. I also switched subject; after theology and medicine, I decided to study philosophy.

My parents were worried about this, given the lack of professional prospects, but supported me. Between four children, though, the support didn't stretch far, so I got a job as a waiter in a guest house in the rural suburb where I lived. I liked the guests, who acknowledged the student waiters with good-natured admiration and generous tips, and I delighted in my skill at balancing ever-increasing numbers of plates and glasses. Sometimes there would be an attempt to run out on a bill, a loud argument, a brawl, a visit from the police. The most exciting thing I experienced as a waiter was a man attacking his wife's lover with a knife; blood was spilled, and the guest house had to stay closed all the following day. Some weeks later, attacker and attacked sat having a beer together; the woman wanted nothing more to do with either of them. I waited tables three nights a week, and with that and my studies and the orchestra, my life was full.

I visited Olga on her birthday, and otherwise every two

or three months. The train journey between my university and my home town was a long one, and a lot of people there had claims on my time: my parents, old friends, the quartet I'd played the flute with for many years. But I would make sure that Olga and I had an afternoon and evening to ourselves. Sometimes we would go and do something together; Olga remained sprightly and curious. Sometimes we spent the afternoon at hers, and in the evening I would take her out to a restaurant. In winter we sat opposite each other in the corners of a sofa in the living-dining room, beneath a watercolour of pine trees, a lake and reeds that she had found in a junk shop and which reminded her of Pomerania. In summer we sat on the balcony, which was just big enough for two chairs. Trucks rumbled and locomotives whistled in the goods yard; the little garden smelled sweet and attracted the bees. I found it idyllic, but on my last visit Olga was unhappy about the view. The water tower had been demolished.

She always gave me something to take with me when I left: a marble cake with chocolate icing that she had baked, jam she had made, or apple slices she had dried. I was touched by this, and every time I found it hard to take my leave. As nimble and strong as Olga was, she was nearly ninety; she might have a fall or her heart might stop or her brain malfunction, and every leave-taking could be the last. We didn't hug each other in greeting or when taking our leave; it wasn't the custom. She stroked my head, as she had stroked my head when I was a child. And that was what she still called me: child.

13

One spring morning I got a call from my mother. Olga was in hospital, she was going to die, I should come at once. My mother said something about an explosion and a serious injury, she couldn't explain the details to me now, I should buy the newspaper at the station.

It was the front-page headline. Sometime in the early hours of Sunday morning, a bomb had gone off in the municipal park in my home town. The attack had targeted the Bismarck monument, which had not been damaged, but it had critically injured a passer-by, who had probably stumbled upon the bombers' preparations and caused them to set off the bomb too soon. This was the third such attack, following attacks on the war memorial in Hamburg and the Kaiser Wilhelm monument in Ems. It was the first in which someone had been injured. The editorial was about the students' path towards radicalism and terrorism. Those who no longer showed any consideration for life and limb must reckon with the worst, it said; the full severity and rigour of the constitutional state must be brought to bear.

My first thought was of Olga and Bismarck. The man

she held responsible for so much would now be responsible for her death. There was something comic, ironic, absurd about this, and I wondered whether Olga, if she could still laugh, had laughed about it. Then I wondered where she had been coming from in the middle of the night, and where she had been going, whether it was on account of her deafness that she hadn't heard and steered clear of the perpetrators, what the nature of her injuries was, whether she was in pain, whether she was being given morphine, whether we would be able to speak to each other. It was only then that what my mother had said on the phone really hit me. Olga was going to die.

I sat on the train, passing through a spring landscape beneath a blue sky, forests in fresh green, fruit trees with pink blossoms, a landscape for hiking or walking. Olga had been looking forward to spring. I had planned to visit her again in three weeks' time.

I knew she wasn't afraid of death. I also knew that I would have to lose her eventually, a little earlier or a little later. She was old. But the understanding she showed me, both curious and indulgent, and her love, which delighted in me without needing me or making demands of me – this I had had with my grandparents, but not with anyone else, not with my parents, not with friends, not with lovers. I was losing something I would never find again. And I was losing the conversations with her, and her face and her form, her warm hands and her smell of lavender. After her death I would never return to my home town, arrive there, the way I had before.

My mother picked me up at the station and drove me straight to the hospital. She prepared me: the explosion had ripped open Olga's side and belly and had damaged her organs so badly that all they could do for her was take the pain away and wait for death. She was on morphine, dozing, sleeping, sometimes conscious, often not, knew that she was dying, and had come to terms with this. She was glad I was coming, but she would probably be asleep when I arrived, and I had to prepare myself for the possibility that she might not wake up.

14

A nurse brought me to Olga's sickbed. She was lying in a single room with the sun shining in through the big window. I looked out over a car park, a little meadow and a row of poplars. She was on a drip; the nurse checked that the clear liquid was flowing evenly into Olga's vein and left.

Olga was asleep. Beside the little table, on which was a big bunch of flowers and a card from the mayor expressing his horror and sympathy and wishing her a swift recovery, stood a chair. I pulled it over to the bed, sat down, took Olga's hand and looked at her.

She had scratches on her face, conspicuous because they had been painted over in red, but not severe. Her skin was grey and wizened, her mouth was open, she was snoring gently, and her eyelids fluttered. She looked as if she'd had a sleepless night or had overexerted herself, not like the victim of a murderous attack. As if a day in the sun, good food and a good night's sleep would put her back to rights.

Her hand lay lightly in mine. I looked at the age spots, the prominent veins, the slender fingers with the bony knuckles, the short, clipped nails. It was her right hand, the hand with which she used to stroke my head. I placed my other hand on hers as if I could protect her.

She opened her eyes. Her gaze wandered for a moment, found me, and her face lit up with such love, such delight, that I couldn't help but weep. I couldn't believe it: that this radiance was for me; that she so loved and delighted in me; that anyone could love and delight in me so.

'Oh, child,' she said, 'oh, child.'

We exchanged a few sentences.

'Are you in pain?'

'No, not at all.'

'Are they treating you well?'

'I'm glad you're here.'

'I'm glad I'm here.'

'Did your mother tell you about me?'

'What happened on Saturday night?'

'Does it matter?'

'You didn't want to die like this.'

'It's not a bad way to die.'

Then her eyes fell shut again, and I went on holding her hand and went on looking at her face. She too had wept; tears clung to her cheeks.

I stayed until the doctor did his rounds. He threw a quick glance at the sleeping Olga, nodded to me, nodded to the nurse, and left again. The nurse hung a fresh bag on the drip, asked me how long Olga had been asleep, and advised me to come back later or the next day. If Olga hadn't woken up when the doctor came by, she wouldn't wake any time soon.

I walked through the town, from bridge to bridge, up one riverbank and back down the other, through the streets and into the fields. I sat down beside the canal and watched the water and the barges. Then I was drawn to the municipal park, to the Bismarck monument. It was cordoned off, but no one was poking around in the gravel or grass for traces of the attack, and Bismarck sat firmly on his high pedestal. I had known it since childhood, pale sandstone on dark, shining granite, the bald head and moustache of the bust like the bald head and moustache of my grandfather. I had never studied the monument more closely. Was it a little lopsided? Or was I just imagining it? And was it only now that it was like that? Or had it always been that way?

At eight o'clock I was back at the hospital. Olga was asleep, as before, and I sat down by her bed again and took her hand again. Sometimes she opened her eyes for a moment or shook her head. Sometimes her mouth made a sound as if it were trying to say something, but they weren't whole words and I couldn't understand anything. Sometimes her hand twitched in mine. Slowly the liquid in the bag dripped down. Slowly it grew dark outside.

At some point I fell asleep. When I woke, Olga's hand lay cold in mine. I found the night nurse, who accompanied me to her bedside. Yes, Olga was dead.

15

She was buried in the Bergfriedhof. A reporter who was writing something about Olga had tracked me down and asked me about her life. I'd told him about her love of the Bergfriedhof, he had mentioned it in his article, and as the victim of a terrorist attack she was sufficiently high-profile to be buried, by order of the mayor, in that place where not everyone was buried.

The only funerals I had been to before this were those of my grandparents. Great crowds of relatives and friends had come to these events; memories of my grandparents had been exchanged and their lives celebrated. At Olga's funeral my mother and I were alone at first, but then one of the mayor's representatives turned up with a big wreath, along with the reporter I had met and a gentleman I didn't know. We stood in the chapel and heard the vicar say what my mother had said to him about Olga, and we stood at the grave and threw our bouquet of colourful roses and our trowelfuls of earth into the grave.

On the way to the car park the gentleman I didn't know addressed me. 'Commissar Welker. Do you have a moment? I didn't want to ask you to come in and see us specially; I just have a couple of questions.'

We stopped.

'There are things about the attack that are puzzling. The impact of the explosion, the type of injury – you might almost think the attack was aimed at the deceased. This is going to sound as strange to you as it does to us, but I have to ask: do you know of any dangerous activities the deceased might, knowingly or unknowingly, have been caught up in?'

I laughed. 'I think she would have been delighted the police thought her capable of doing anything dangerous. But it's completely out of the question. You do know that she was deaf?'

He nodded. 'Can you imagine what she might have been doing in the municipal park between two and three a.m. on Sunday morning?'

'I asked her, but she didn't feel like answering. She had hardly any strength left to speak, and she didn't think it was important. She liked to walk; perhaps she couldn't sleep. She never said anything about it, but I can imagine her going for walks around town on sleepless nights. She wasn't afraid of anything.'

Commissar Welker thanked me and left. My mother had been listening to our conversation. 'If she'd been in the habit of doing that, she would have mentioned it at some point.'

I shrugged. 'I think so, too. But what do I know?' I'd thought I'd known her. But her late-night walk in the municipal park was a mystery, and a habit of taking late-night walks around town was still the best explanation.

I spent that night at my parents' house before heading back to university the next day. Clearing out her apartment, stopping bank accounts, insurance policies, memberships, subscriptions – I was really the one who owed it to Olga to do this, but my exams were coming up, so my mother took over for me. On Monday we went to Olga's apartment and made a note of the things I'd like to keep: the watercolour with the pines and the lake and the reeds, books, papers, the jewellery I liked seeing Olga wear. My mother would deal with her estate.

A few weeks later I received a letter from the probate court. Olga had appointed me her legal heir. There were twelve thousand marks in her savings account. I didn't want to touch the money. I transferred the savings book into my name, put it away with my birth certificate, confirmation certificate and school certificates and forgot about it.

16

I completed my studies with a Ph.D. on Rousseau's philosophical and pedagogical novel *Émile*. The evaluation did not suggest that I should become a professor, as I would have liked. However, there were state ministers of cultural affairs, keen on reform, who were seeking to recruit not just teachers and lawyers but outsiders as well, so I started work at the ministry. It was at the ministry that I met my wife. When I became a civil servant, we got married; soon afterwards we had our two children and built our house. The easy and difficult phases of our marriage, our delight in our children and our worries about them – this was the pattern of our life. Fate spared us its blows, and we never had reason to fear the coming day.

I stayed at the ministry and was, over the years, responsible for school statistics, requirements planning, task scheduling, personnel planning and development, recruitment and transfers, and free schools; by the time I retired, I was a department head. Sometimes I regretted not becoming a teacher and working with children directly. I worked for them indirectly, though. And I enjoyed my frame of activity: I entered it happily each morning, I knew how things worked there, and I left each evening feeling satisfied. Afterwards, though, no one needed me any more. In that respect, doctors and lawyers, who help out their successors a bit after they retire, and managers and engineers, who are in demand as advisors, have it better.

My wife was still working as an administrator, so I took over the chores I'd never really contributed to properly: shopping, cooking and washing up, the laundry, the garden. At first my wife was delighted by my evening displays of culinary expertise, and by the fact that the laundry retained its colours, jerseys didn't lose their shape and blouses weren't wrinkled. After she grew accustomed to it, sitting down at the table just as exhausted and taciturn and taking her clothes out of the wardrobe just as casually as I had done for decades, I stopped enjoying it. I continued to enjoy the garden. By growing and blossoming and bearing berries, flowers and bushes reward the gardener, even if his exhausted, taciturn wife doesn't praise him. But I was looking forward to the day when my wife would stop working. We would share the work in the house and garden and would finally go on those trips we had dreamed of to the north: to the Hebrides, to Scotland and Scandinavia, Canada and Alaska.

It didn't turn out like that. A few months before her retirement – we had been horrified to read in the paper that morning about an arson attack on a refugee hostel – my wife was driving in freezing rain, had an accident, and died on the way to the hospital. I wasn't able to say goodbye to her.

Since then, I've lived alone. The house is too big, but I'm attached to it, and I manage. My son is an architect; he builds in China, and when he's in Germany he lives with me. My daughter is a teacher in a nearby town, married, a mother of three who take it in turns to visit me in the holidays. I have every reason to be thankful for my life, despite the pain of losing my wife. I'm attached to people and places, I need permanence, I hate rifts, I have led and continue to lead a constant life.

And I was, and am, constantly reminded of Olga.

17

And not only because the photographs of my loved ones on the wall beside my desk include the photograph of Olga that she had taken after her escape from the East. I found it under her papers with the photograph of Viktoria, Herbert and her taken the day before their confirmation, the diplomas from her teacher training course and the school for the deaf, a sketch, signed by Eik, of the facade and floor plan of a school, and a bundle of letters from Herbert in German South-West Africa.

Whenever I come to my home town – which, since my parents died, isn't regularly, but occasionally, for school reunions and to meet friends – I walk past the Bismarck monument. I've examined it often and carefully, and I'm sure now that it's slightly lopsided. It's still Bismarck, but his lopsidedness means that, for me, it's a monument to Olga.

Whenever I go on a walk or a hike with someone and we don't speak, or whenever I come out of the cinema with someone and we wait a while before talking about the film, I think of Olga. Also when someone happily tells me that they have found the person with whom they can be silent. It feels good to have a connection with another and not have to perform or entertain them. But this isn't something some can do and others can't, that connects some and separates others. Silence can be learned; like waiting, which is a part of silence.

The pleasure of walking in cemeteries is another thing I've inherited from Olga, and when it's a particularly special cemetery, particularly old or particularly beautiful, enchanted or eerie, I take her with me in my imagination. We were closest in the cemetery I liked to visit when I was on holiday in rural America. It lay all alone in a forest, a flat meadow that turned into small hills covered with grass and crowned with trees. First the Indians buried their dead here, then the settlers of the eighteenth and nineteenth centuries, before the dead were buried in the meadow as well. It had no plots, only gravestones, big ones for adults and small ones for children, many of them bearing the same names, English, Dutch, German, sometimes the dead person's profession and commendable qualities; on one a slave who had fled from the South to the North had noted the year of his freedom; many bore little American flags that indicated a war veteran. Everyone lay together, from the Indians who had died of the past to people of today who had died of the present. It was a place of equality, and death had lost its horror.

I also can't watch any film on DVD or download one from the internet without thinking how happy Olga would be to be able to switch on subtitles for every film. Good as she was at lip-reading and working things out from the screen, her greatest joy was foreign films with German subtitles. I can't see paintings by Feuerbach and Böcklin or *The Execution of Emperor Maximilian* without thinking of her, or any fountain pen, or any sewing machine, especially old ones.

And she comes to my mind when something happens that I know she would regard as getting too grand. She had thought we students were getting above ourselves with our moralizing – nowadays she would scoff at the media that have forgotten how to do research and replaced it with moralizing sensationalism. In Berlin, she would find the Chancellery and the Bundestag building and the Holocaust memorial too grand. She would be pleased about German reunification, but she would find the newly enlarged Europe too big, and the globalized world as well.

18

At times I was reminded of Herbert, too.

One Sunday, a long time ago now, when the children were still small, my wife and I were walking with them through a big flea market, and among the crockery and cutlery, brass lamps and Bakelite fountain pens, handbags and hand towels, I found, in a box of old postcards, a series entitled 'German Horsemen in South-West Africa', with coloured pictures of members of the colonial force on horseback and on foot, sometimes on a hill with a view off into the distance, sometimes taking cover beneath the crest of a dune, sometimes driving up with a cannon or a machine gun, often charging with a raised sabre or fixed bayonet; finally, mouths agape, singing at the Christmas party with an African tree and metallic stars. Two pictures show them in battle; in one they are lying on a rocky plateau, shooting, small white clouds emerging from the muzzles of their rifles; in the other they are riding towards a few Herero. These German horsemen in South-West Africa, with their sand-grey uniforms and dark-grey hats, brim jauntily turned up on the right with a black, white and red cockade, their moustaches twirled into points

– they look almost dapper. And I could imagine them setting German hearts aflutter.

I thought of Herbert, too, when I read about the Ovambos' struggle for liberation, and about Namibian independence, and again when American and Soviet submarines broke through the ice and surfaced at the North Pole and a Soviet icebreaker made it through the North-East Passage in eighteen days. Would Herbert have been angry, or Olga happy, that the story rendered his endeavours superfluous?

Then I read in the paper about an expedition that had set off for Nordaustlandet to find out what had happened to Herbert all those years ago. It was an opportunity to commemorate Herbert's life, his deployment in Africa and his Arctic ambitions, the madness of the poorly prepared expedition to Nordaustlandet that had set out too late, its failure, and the unsuccessful attempts by several rescue expeditions to save Herbert and the three companions with whom he set out to cross the island. There was also mention of various pieces of equipment: an aluminium saucepan picked up by a Norwegian seal hunter in 1937, and aluminium plates German soldiers came across in 1945.

The expedition found no trace of Herbert. Just as a man who loses his key can only search for it under the streetlamp because it's only under the streetlamp that he has enough light to search, the expedition could only search where the terrain was suitable for searching, not on the ice caps and glaciers where Herbert may have strayed. The expedition report described efficient solar modules, encounters with reindeer and polar bears, and sledge rides, mostly laborious toil through pack ice or grease ice, sometimes rushes of joy. The pictures showed blue sky, white snow, red tents, sledges laden with red cargo, huskies with red tongues and cheerful, heavily bundled-up people.

I had pictured the Arctic differently, as a chasm of gloom, the nothingness in which Herbert's longing had lost itself. The books I found in the university library about Herbert's expedition had black-and-white pictures where everything is indeed gloomy: grey snow and sky, the men and dogs dark silhouettes, the landscape indistinct, craggy, inhospitable. A member of Herbert's expedition who made it back concluded his notes with a sigh about the unfathomable workings of cruel nature, bowing down before her in silent, horrified awe.

19

An expedition that didn't find what it sought, and a few postcards, designed to inspire nationalist feelings: how strange, the things that end up determining our path!

Six months after the expedition report was published, I received a letter from a certain Adelheid Volkmann in Berlin, requesting a meeting. Her father had told her about Herbert Schröder and Olga Rinke, and a newspaper report had prompted her to resume the search for Olga Rinke, which had previously been abandoned as hopeless. This time she had engaged a detective agency, and that was how she had come across me as Olga Rinke's heir.

At the same time, I received an email from Robert Kurz in Sinsheim, another postcard collector. The pictures of the German horsemen in South-West Africa had awakened my enthusiasm for old postcards. My wife loved flea markets, and while she looked around, open to anything, I would sift through old postcards in boxes. These days, I'm familiar with the world of postcard collectors; I know that they specialize in subjects, events and locations, I know their journals, meetings, swap meets, websites and chat rooms, and the criteria that determine a postcard's value and price. I didn't become a serious collector. Serious collectors specialize, and particularly ambitious collectors even hope for completeness: every single postcard of the Kyffhäuser monument or the Golden Gate Bridge, for example. I collected postcards I liked. I also paid attention to what was written on the back. Serious collectors are contemptuous of this, but I like it when the postcards tell a story.

In my collection I have a postcard of the Boston Light lighthouse, on which a mother warns her son in Casablanca in September 1918 that there's a deadly influenza outbreak and he should delay his return to Boston. In October 1926, Gilbert in Belfast sent his friend Haakon in Oslo a picture of a full wine glass, urging him not to miss voting in the referendum while on holiday; he would only come and visit if prohibition in Norway were repealed. A postcard from June 1936 shows Napoleon on St Helena; on it, James in St Helena sends greetings to his brother Phil in Oxford, and writes that he has found traces of arsenic in the earth where Napoleon was buried before being transferred to Paris. I also have an old postcard of the Bismarck monument on which the pedestal and bust stand upright. But I digress.

Three years ago, I found a postcard of the German Reichstag from May 1913, sent to Peter Goldbach in Tromsø, poste restante. The dealer couldn't remember where he'd got the postcard. I advertised everywhere postcard collectors advertise. Who knew someone who was offering postcards sent to Tromsø poste restante in 1913/1914? The tips I got weren't helpful, but I remained undeterred and kept renewing the advertisements. A few days after receiving Adelheid Volkmann's letter, the email arrived from Robert Kurz. His son had just brought back for him from a Norwegian cruise a bunch of postcards he'd found in a second-hand bookshop in Tromsø, all with addressees in Tromsø, poste restante. His son couldn't remember the name of the bookshop.

A second-hand bookshop in Tromsø was listed on the internet. I called, asked questions in English and got English answers. It wasn't here that the son had found the postcards. Were there other second-hand bookshops in Tromsø? One, but the owner was in the process of reorganizing and renovating and wasn't properly open for business yet. They were sorry, but they couldn't help with a name or an address or a telephone number.

I wrote to Adelheid Volkmann suggesting we meet in two weeks' time, and gave her my telephone number and email. I booked a ticket and flew to Oslo two days later, and from there on to Tromsø.

20

It was dark in Tromsø when I woke in the morning, and I realized that I couldn't expect anything else in January; a faint light at midday at most. I went over to the window and looked out across a harbour with lights and small and large ships, other hotels with flat roofs and smooth facades, and a square covered in dirty snow. The previous evening, a bus had conveyed me through snowy countryside and a long tunnel from the airport into town, down a brightly lit street with shops and restaurants to my hotel on a side street. The brightly lit street must be the main street; there had to be a place on it where I could find a map of the city and ask about the second-hand bookshop.

It was on one of the streets on the hill, I was told, if it was already open. So I walked around the streets on the hill, saw a church, a university campus, office buildings, residential buildings, a flower shop belonging to a garden centre, and a shop whose windows no longer displayed items for sale but women and men sitting at computers. At midday I ate in a restaurant on the main street, then went back to the streets on the hill. It was snowing, and I placed my feet slowly and carefully on the slippery, snow-covered pavement.

I found the second-hand bookshop just as the grey of midday was again giving way to darkness. It was in the basement of an apartment building; steps led down to the door and the windows were at ground level. Stuck on them were big white transparent letters – *ANTIKVARIAT* – and between the letters I could see the bookseller shelving books. I greeted him as I entered, and he greeted me; that was all. The bookseller had no other customers, but he didn't turn to me and didn't ask if I was looking for something and whether he could help me. He gave me a searching look, his face unfriendly, mistrustful, and turned back to the books.

I went along the shelves. Sometimes I recognized the name of an author and was able to work out the title; I also understood *geografi* and *historie*, but apart from that I capitulated before the foreign language. On a table sat boxes of old postcards from all over the world, sorted by country. I picked out one after another and checked the address. Tromsø, poste restante.

I didn't know how to proceed. Could I simply ask where he had got all these postcards sent poste restante to Tromsø? And whether there were also any letters sent poste restante to Tromsø? Whether I might look through the letters? How much he wanted for a letter? Would we even understand each other?

I asked the bookseller in English for German books, and he directed me, in English, to a shelf of German literature in the next room. I found geographical, geological and biological texts, and novels from the thirties and forties; the books had probably been left behind after the occupation. In the middle of the room was a table with two armchairs, and on the table I found more boxes; not old postcards this time but old letters, again addressed to Tromsø, poste restante.

I went back to the bookseller. 'You have a lot of interesting things.'

'Glad you think so. I'd like to have a wider selection, but I'm just starting out.'

'You have a wide range of old postcards and letters.'

'Yes. Customers often come just for the letters. I don't know what I'd do without people's voyeuristic pleasure in letters from the past and their long-forgotten writers.'

'Where did you get them?'

He laughed. 'That's my secret.'

'Do you have more?'

'Enough to fill the boxes for years.'

The obvious thing now was to get around to talking about Olga's letters. But he had mentioned his secret, and I wanted to get to the bottom of it first. At least I knew he had letters, and that we could speak to each other in English. So I said, 'I'll be back,' and left. A sign on the door said: 'ÅPNINGSTIDER 14:00–20:00'.

21

The next day I waited until evening. I wandered around the streets of the old town with its wooden houses and churches; in the harbour, I looked out at the shimmering grey sea and the grey bridge that stretches in a high arc from the island where Tromsø is situated to the mainland. I threw bread to the seagulls; they snatched it up mid-flight and carried it away. I walked over the grey bridge, the wind whistling through the railings; I took a cable car up a mountain, stood in the snow and saw the town and the sea below me.

Enough poste restante sent to Tromsø to fill the boxes for years – there was something fishy about this. I'd been a civil servant; uncollected poste restante had to be either brought to the post office archive or destroyed. To do anything else would in the past have simply been sloppy, and nowadays it was incompatible with personal and data protection.

I entered the bookshop shortly before eight. The bookseller was just putting on his coat. 'Are you leaving? I need to talk to you.'

He stood there, undecided, and gave me a surly look

before eventually removing his coat again. 'I think I can spare a moment.'

'Close the shop and let's go into the other room.' I sat down in one of the two armchairs, took the bottle of bourbon and the two glasses I'd bought out of my bag and poured us both a measure. He sat down, and I raised my glass. 'To good business!'

'I don't know—'

'Drink!' We drank, and in his face I saw the unfriendly, mistrustful look I had noticed the previous day – but also greed.

'I don't know whether you have what I'm looking for. Perhaps you've never had it, or have already sold it. But perhaps it might turn up in your treasure trove of Tromsø poste restante.' I told him about Olga Rinke and Herbert Schröder.

'What are the letters worth to you?'

'Do you have them?'

'I don't know. I'd have to search through what you call my treasure trove. That's a lot of work; it'll take a long time. So, again: what are the letters worth to you?'

'One hundred euros per letter.'

'One hundred euros?' He shook his head, laughing. 'If they're not worth a thousand to you—'

'In that case, I'd rather go to the people from the post office archive and hope they'll let me look through the treasure trove once they've recovered it from you.'

'And what if they don't let you look through it?'

'Then I'll have had bad luck. That's why I'd like to do business with you. But it has to work for both of us.'

'Five hundred.'

'Two hundred.'

We agreed on three hundred, and he told me how he had acquired the treasure.

'Do you know the old post office? Soon to be the new library? The building had a huge attic, and instead of giving the uncollected poste restante to the post office archive, as they should have done, the postmasters stored it up there. It was easy, and there was always something more important to do than packing the stuff up and sending it off. Once the new post office was ready and the old one was being cleared out and handed over, it was a bit late for that. So they wanted to get rid of the old mail. Secretly, of course. A friend who works at the post office promised he would deal with it, and we dealt with it and cleared the attic.' He got up and unlocked the door to the next room, a cellar full of letters, individual and bundled, in small and large envelopes, along with small and large packets, and postcards.

I went and stood beside him. 'Shouldn't I look through this? You have plenty of other things to do.'

'So you can find twenty letters and pocket ten and show me ten? How dumb do you think I am?'

'I could—'

'You could nothing. I'd have to body-search you every time. No, I'll look through the mail, and if I find something, send me the money and I'll send you the letters. And I'd like a thousand now for searching, in case I don't find any letters, and if I do find some, you can send me the balance.'

'How long will you need?'

'A few weeks, one or two months, maybe three – as you say, I've got plenty of other things to do. I'll do it as fast as I can.'

'Two thousand, and no longer than two months.'

He nodded, I topped up our glasses, and we toasted the deal.

The next day I withdrew two thousand euros from the bank, brought them to him, and flew home.

22

I still hadn't accomplished anything. But the travelling and the finding and the haggling and setting the search for the letters in motion and getting a fair price had invigorated me. Was I living too cautiously the rest of the time? Ought I to be more courageous?

I remembered the fox I'd seen in the zoo in my home town when I was a child. It was a small zoo, and the canopied wire enclosure in which the fox ran ceaselessly from left to right and from right to left was small as well. As it turned, it always pushed off with the same paw from the same dark, worn-down, gleaming patch on the enclosure's concrete base. Was I too leaving only a dark, worn-down, gleaming patch? Or not even that?

I'm just an ordinary man with an ordinary life. I haven't achieved anything great. I have an eye for the greatness of others, and would have been a good chronicler of a Faustian friend. I had no such friend. But I had Olga; my memories of her were precious to me, and it was enough for me to be her chronicler.

It had taken me to Tromsø, and it brought me the visit from Adelheid Volkmann.

We spoke on the phone a few times. Should she fly or take the train, book the hotel by the river or the guest house near me? She opted for the train and the guest house, and I puzzled as to why. Did she like the idea of a relaxed train journey and staying near my house, or did she not have much money? Was she thrifty, or tight-fisted? The saver ticket on the train was cheaper than a flight, and the guest house cheaper than the hotel. And what was she like otherwise? Her voice sounded youthful, but old women can have young voices, and her speaking calmly could indicate a relaxed personality, or a slow or boring one.

I picked her up at the station, and because it was a February day with spring in the air and people were sitting in street cafés and beer gardens in their shirtsleeves, I drove her to a garden restaurant by the river. We had an hour of sunshine left, enough for a tea.

We sat down, and I looked at her, the wrinkles around her eyes and mouth, the grey-blond hair, the green eyes, the large mouth. She was probably around sixty. Her skin was withered, as if she smoked or had done until recently, and she wasn't wearing any make-up. Walking from the train platform to the car and from the car to the restaurant – I a little taller than her, she a little fatter than me – I'd noticed her confident, assertive step. And this was how she was, sitting opposite me: confident and assertive.

'Have you just given up smoking? When you took the paper handkerchief out of its packet just now, you held the packet out to me for a moment the way a smoker would hold out a pack of cigarettes.'

She laughed. 'Did I? Yes, I've given up. I was afraid I wouldn't be able to write without them, but I can.

When I was at the newspaper, I never wrote without a cigarette, even if I forgot about it and it burned down in the ashtray. When the same thing happened there as everywhere else – falling circulation, collapsing advertising revenue, redundancies – I said goodbye not just to the newspaper but to smoking as well. That was five weeks ago. Since then, I've been writing freelance and hoping I can make a living from it.'

I asked more questions, and by the time we left I knew how she had stopped smoking, that she wrote about gardens, food and health, had an allotment, was divorced, that her daughter and granddaughter lived in America, that she translated poems from English into German and enjoyed living alone. She asked me questions, too, and by the time we left she knew all about my circumstances.

'May I invite you to dinner at my place? The good restaurants are all crowded and loud, which makes it difficult for me to hear. I'm not a bad cook.'

She accepted, I dropped her off at the guest house and described the short walk to my house. 'See you at eight.'

23

I had already prepared dinner: cauliflower soup, beef stroganoff, baked apples; I didn't have to start cooking right away, I could sit down and think for a bit. Who did Adelheid Volkmann remind me of? What was it about her that reminded me? Her face, her youthful voice, her calm way of speaking, her confident, assertive manner? At least I understood why she had to economize.

I'd thought we would eat first and then talk, but she started while we were still on our aperitifs. 'My father returned from captivity in Russia in 1955 – one of the last. He'd got married in 1939; my mother had my brother in 1940, and in 1956 she was still young enough to have me. Things didn't go well between my parents; she'd managed without him for fifteen years and didn't need him, he hadn't had a woman in fifteen years, hadn't harassed any either, and he wanted to make up for that, and he didn't know what to do with my brother, who'd dropped the name Adolf and was calling himself Dolf instead. He focused on me. He told me about the war and captivity, why he'd fallen in love with my mother and why he shouldn't have fallen in love with her, why he couldn't stand her any more and was having an affair with the neighbour. I was flattered; I felt taken seriously and loved. It was only after his death that I realized he'd used me. He wasn't good for me. He was a police detective, incidentally, the head of the criminal investigation department when he retired. Died of lung cancer in 1972.' She smiled. 'He was the one who introduced me to smoking, too.'

She took a sip, shook her head and stared into space. I was about to remind her of dinner when she continued talking. 'When everyone was rebelling against their parents, I rebelled against my dead father. His egotism, his bigotry, his bragging, his behaviour towards his wife and us children – there was more than enough. I knew that he'd lied about his past; there were too many things that didn't fit together. He claimed to have studied architecture, but was with the criminal investigation department; he—'

'Was his name Eik?'

'Good, so you know something about him. His parents and siblings must have died during the expulsion from East Prussia; he made enquiries through the tracing service, all in vain. But there was this aunt, Olga Rinke, who was very fond of him, and he was very fond of her; he'd lived with her for a long time when he was a child, after the war, and she'd told him lots of stories about her friend Herbert Schröder, which he then told me. My father loved German heroes.'

'He only died in 1972? Olga Rinke was still alive then.'

'But the two of them don't seem to have been in touch. Why? And is there anything about my father in her will? What was he like as a child, and as a young man? Did he really study architecture, and what did he do with it, and how did he end up a detective? Are the things he told me about the seventeen-year-old girl he married true?'

She gave me a questioning look. Eik's daughter. The last thing Olga had told me about Eik was about his visits to her after she lost her hearing. After that, he had simply dropped out of her stories. Why had I never wondered about that?

'Do you know what Olga Rinke looked like?' I took her into my study and showed her the photograph.

She looked at it for a long time, and then at the others on the wall. 'Is that your wife? Are those your children? Who's that?'

I introduced her to my wife and my children, my parents and siblings, my friends, and also to the black cat with white paws that my daughter was given at the age of twelve, which had stayed with us for seventeen years. 'Shall we eat? I can tell you what little I know over dinner.'

24

I started with what I knew about Eik, his parents, his journey from the farm to Tilsit and Berlin and Italy, his entry into the Party and the SS, Olga's role in his life and his visits to her. Then she wanted to hear about Olga and Herbert, their childhood and their love, his colonial and Arctic dreams, his expedition to Nordaustlandet, her poste restante letters. Finally, she wanted to know how Olga and I had got to know each other and become close.

I talked through the starter, the main dish, the dessert. When I finished I apologized for talking for so long.

'No, no, I kept on asking questions.' She traced circles on the tablecloth with her wine glass. 'Father in the Party and the SS – it would have been nice if things had been different, but I thought it must have been something like that. It fits. What you told me about him and Olga . . . I don't understand it. She was devoted to him and looked after him, and I can't see why Father would have lied when he said he lived with her for a long time. Did they have contact after the war that we don't know about? Why did they keep it secret?'

'I don't know.' I carried the dishes into the kitchen.

When I came back, she was still playing with her wine glass. 'What did your mother say?'

'My mother?' She started out of her reverie. 'She never mentioned Olga. When Father was a prisoner of war she hardly said anything about him, and soon after he came back she only said nasty things. She got dementia not long before he died. She should have left him, sooner rather than later; she was a nurse, she didn't need him financially. But divorce was out of the question for her.'

She got up, looked out of the window into the night, walked up and down the room, ran her eyes over my books and my CDs and turned to the picture that hung between the shelves, Jean-Jacques Rousseau in fur hat and kaftan, a late eighteenth-century print.

She asked, 'Was there a rift between the two of them? Why?'

'You can't ask me that. I don't understand anything about rifts.'

'What is there to understand? If it doesn't work any more, it doesn't work, and you separate.'

'Yes, you said you were divorced.'

She answered the question I didn't dare ask. 'He was a painter, perhaps a genius, I don't know. At first I liked his obsessiveness. But he paid no attention to anything apart from his art, and I was responsible for money and for Jana and for the house, an old farm he'd inherited on the edge of the Teutoburg Forest that was falling apart. After a few years I couldn't do it any more. And I couldn't stand him any more, either, this narcissistic child, bigger than Jana but more troublesome. Breaking up with him wasn't hard for me.'

'I can't bear rifts. I've stayed in touch with everyone

I've been connected to over the course of my life, and, bumpy as our marriage was, divorce was out of the question for me, too.'

'How did Olga Rinke deal with rifts? Did she find them hard? Easy?'

'I don't know. I thought I knew her. But until she died I had no idea about her nocturnal walks, and until hearing your story I knew she'd looked after Eik, but not that he lived with her for years. I'm guessing those were the years when the village where his parents lived was occupied by the French or the Lithuanians and he was at high school in Tilsit. There were no rifts in our relationship, and I thought Olga was as constant as me. But apparently not.'

She nodded. She knew that others are not as we think they are. 'Thank you for this evening, the dinner, all you've told me. Tomorrow I'm going to research an article about last year's horticultural show so I can put the trip on expenses. Do you feel like coming with me?'

I promised to pick her up in the car at nine o'clock, and I walked her back to her guest house two streets away.

25

When I meet confident, assertive people like her, and also learn that they find committing and detaching themselves easy, I don't want to even begin to get involved with them: I already know that they'll leave me. But there was an easy familiarity between us on the drive to the Black Forest; we each talked about ourselves as if we really wanted to discover the other, we used the informal *du* form of address, and when we were silent, there was no need for speech.

The mayor had used the horticultural show to restore some sparkle to the town, which had seen better days, having lost its industries and its rich citizens: a park around the remains of the old castle, a fresh bed for the little river that had been bricked over, a riverbank promenade. The residents had joined in, putting flower boxes in their windows that promised a rich display of blooms in summer, and the sun shone on many a freshly plastered house. The last vestiges of snow were turning grey in shaded corners. Adelheid had a camera with her and was taking photographs.

'Winter after the Horticultural Show' was the title of

the article she was writing for *Park and Garden*. She had set up interviews with the mayor, the director of the horticultural show and the editor-in-chief of the local newspaper, and I sat in on them and saw how good she was at her job. She was well informed and friendly, and doggedly persistent when they tried to dodge questions about the follow-up costs and debts incurred. The mayor insisted on inviting us to dinner at the Golden Swan, which had acquired a new manager and a new cook for the horticultural show and was now promoting the city on the gastronomic front as well.

We left later than we had intended. The day had started out warm and sunny, like the day before. In the afternoon the weather had turned, the temperature had dropped and the blue sky had gone grey. As we stepped out of the Golden Swan into the night and headed for the car, a few snowflakes started to fall.

I drove off fast. I thought that if it was snowing we'd be better off on the autobahn than on the country road, and I could reach the autobahn before the snow got any heavier. But after just a few kilometres it was already falling so heavily that the windscreen wipers could only move with difficulty, and I too had to drive slowly. I could hardly see a thing. The white road, white crash barrier and white embankment blurred into one another, the snowflakes refracted the light from the headlamps, and oncoming cars only became visible right at the last moment. Sometimes the wheels spun and we skidded, but recovered. We passed a car that had got stuck in the ditch by the side of the road. The driver waved us on; if we had stopped on that uphill slope we probably wouldn't have been able to get going again.

Adelheid and I didn't talk. I sat, tensed up, staring into the white flurry and clutching the steering wheel tighter than necessary. Until she placed her hand on my shoulder and said, 'I like this. This cold outside, and the warmth inside, the slowness. It doesn't matter if we don't get back till midnight.'

I nodded, but it took a while before I finally relaxed and was able to ask, 'What else did Eik say about Olga? What was she like? Strict? Indulgent? Did she try to educate him, or did she leave that to his parents?'

'For a long time, I forgave Father everything. I thought that after fifteen years of war and captivity a man just wants to live, and if his wife rejects him, he needs a lover. It was only much later, only when Mother already had dementia, that he told me he'd already been unfaithful to her when they were young newlyweds and she was pregnant, that he hadn't even hidden it from her.' She sighed. 'Because Mother, in her dementia, was such a stranger to me by then, I even forgave him for this. It was only after her death that I could sympathize with that young woman and understand what he had done to her and what she'd suffered.' She sighed again. 'But you're asking about Olga. From what he told me, I imagined a loving, determined woman, who could tell wonderful tales and whose stories always had a moral. Herbert among the Indians: something about a wound and trust, I can't piece it together any more. Herbert among the Herero: he didn't really look, and you must look at others closely; the more other they are, the closer you need to look. Herbert in the Arctic: big undertakings should be well planned and well prepared. I don't know whether the moral was always Olga's, or sometimes Father's.'

We got home long after midnight. Adelheid hadn't felt it necessary to ask for a front door key that morning, and the guest house had no night porter, so she accepted the offer of my guest room. She was hungry; I reheated the beef stroganoff, made a salad, and we ate, saying little.

'Thank you for everything.' We stood up; she came to me, put her arms around my neck and her head on my chest, and I held her. 'I have to leave tomorrow at six. It's a short night. Will you come to my bed?' She raised her head and looked at me, and when I didn't answer immediately, she laid her head on my chest again.

'I . . . if it's good, I won't be able to bear it that you'll be gone again in the morning. And if it's not good, I don't want it.'

'I understand.' She laughed quietly. 'Perhaps I'll come again and stay longer. Or perhaps you'll come to Berlin.' Then she gently disengaged herself, said, 'Sleep well,' and went to her room.

26

I heard nothing from Tromsø in March. I considered calling and asking how it was going, but left it. If the prospect of money didn't motivate the bookseller to conduct his search, my call wouldn't either.

Adelheid and I wrote to and phoned each other. She sent me the draft of her article, and I sent her the plans for redesigning my garden. She sent me photographs of Eik and her mother, and of herself as a child and young girl. We exchanged opinions on books, music and films, how she preferred to holiday in the south and I in the north, that she would like to have a dog again, I a cat.

As a child, too, and as a young girl, Adelheid reminded me of someone. One of my sisters? Emilie? My wife, whom I hadn't known as a child or young girl but had seen in photographs? One of the children or young girls I'd played or danced with, or had a crush on? In the basement I had a box of old photographs, and wanted to get it to compare them, but I didn't get around to it.

The letter arrived from Tromsø in mid-April. The bookseller had found thirty-one letters and one postcard to

Herbert Schröder. After deducting the upfront payment, he expected a further seven thousand six hundred euros, to be transferred to his account with a bank in London. He would despatch the items once this had been received. If I wanted them sent by courier, I should transfer an additional one hundred and twenty euros.

This was far more money than I had just lying around. As I considered how I might raise this much cash, I remembered Olga's savings book. I took it to the bank, and the twelve thousand marks had turned into more than sixteen thousand euros, more than enough for the transfer.

It was another two weeks before the courier brought me the large envelope at eleven o'clock one Wednesday. Inside were a second envelope, and a letter from the bookseller with no date, no salutation, no greeting, just a signature.

Sorry you had to wait. It wasn't only that I had a lot to do. At first I couldn't work my way through the mountain of letters without repeatedly picking one up and reading it. Then it became an addiction. I found one letter that told a tale of jealousy, and one about a feud between two brothers; I was fascinated, and wanted more. I found a letter from the time of the occupation that revealed a drama of perfidy and betrayal, and one from the time after liberation, in which the writer, a collaborator, announced his suicide. I studied history, you understand, and I thought I would finally be able to grasp the past as it really was. Instead, after another thirty or forty letters, my greedy invasion of other lives disgusted me.

History is not the past as it really was. It's the shape we give it. I wish you more joy of your letters than I had of mine.

Aksel Helland

27

At the top of the envelope lay a bundle of Olga's letters to Herbert. Even without undoing the thin blue thread that tied them together, I could see that there were twenty-five letters from the years 1913 to 1915, chronologically ordered, the oldest at the bottom, the most recent at the top. To my astonishment I found more letters from Olga to Herbert from the thirties, fifties and seventies. There was a letter from Herbert's father dated 10 August 1913, and a postcard from a friend in January 1914 with a picture of the Imperial Palace in Vienna.

Old chap,

I hear from Erwin that you're gadding about in the ice and snow. What the blazes! I've been transferred to Vienna. The balls are starting and we need every dancer we can find. Leave the Eskimo women, come and shake a leg over here!

Your old friend Moritz

The letter from his father, whose name was embossed on the heavy notepaper and envelope, was an emblem of futility.

My son,

Since you left us and went to Berlin, your mother has been ill. She has always had a weak chest, and this is not her first inflammation of the lungs. But her fever, shortness of breath, expectoration and pain have never been this bad.

I am afraid she is going to die. I never leave her bedside.

When she speaks, her words are addressed to you. Come back. Take over the estate and the factory, marry, have children. Let us see young life again here. Sometimes one must take a blow in order to understand. We understand now that what matters is not what we think, but what you want.

Come soon.

Your Father

The letter was written in black, upright, broad handwriting; the nib had scratched, leaving tiny ink blots and slipping to make a hook in the signature. Had the father written the letter in great agitation? Or in great haste, because he hoped that the letter, sent immediately, would reach Herbert before he set off for Nordaustlandet?

I had no clear image of Herbert's parents. I knew from

Olga's stories that they were very attached to Herbert. To him, or to the bearer of the family name and inheritance? Did both parents share the same view? His father had signed the letter not 'Your parents' but 'Your Father'; had he long differed from Herbert's mother in his view of their son's marriage, and had finally persuaded her to agree?

If the letter had reached Herbert, would it have changed his and Olga's destiny? Would Olga have accepted the role of unwanted daughter-in-law? Would she have wanted to live with Herbert and their children under the noses of her parents-in-law? Would Herbert have given up his dreams and become a settled, reliable lord of the manor and factory owner?

What might have been, had things been different – it was neither here nor there. This wasn't what determined whether Olga's life had unfolded as it was supposed to, or had been a mistake. Yet it preoccupied me.

28

With Olga's letters I took my time. The thread around them was tied in a bow; I meant to undo it but I pulled the wrong way, and because I didn't realize it at first, I kept drawing the knot tighter. I didn't use a knife or scissors; I picked the knot apart, untangling the loops and ends, and finally managed to pull the thread out of its knot and away from the bundle, long and thin and blue.

I laid the letters out on the big dining table, five rows of five letters. The envelopes were white; the handwriting, with the Soennecken fountain pen's thin upward and thick downward strokes, was blue, the stamps with Germania's head in profile were colourful, one red ten-pfennig stamp, or combinations of grey and brown two-, three- and five-pfennig stamps. In the top left-hand corner she had written 'Poste restante'. The first letter was written on 29 August 1913, the last on 31 December 1915. The second letter, dated 31 August 1913, was marked 'Read first!' I laid out the letters from the thirties to the seventies in a sixth row.

I went into the kitchen and fetched a kitchen knife with a sharp, pointed blade that I could use to open the envelopes without damaging them further. Starting with the last, I slit the envelope, took out the letter and stroked it flat, and by the time I had opened the first, the written pages and slit envelopes lay beside each other in two neat piles.

With one of the letters I found a photograph. Olga was sitting on a chair, a smile on her face and her hands in her lap; beside her stood a boy of about ten with wide, frightened eyes. I knew her as a girl in the garden, and as a mature woman after her flight; this was the first photograph of her as a young woman. She was not pretty; her face was not sweet or charming, but it had openness and clarity, and Viktoria was right, her prominent cheekbones gave her a slightly Slavic look. In this picture, too, her hair was pulled back in a bun.

I didn't want to start reading just yet. I felt as if I had an appointment with Olga; as if she would be here soon, but I would have to wait a while longer. And so I waited for her, and thought about the girl and young woman I hadn't met, of Fräulein Rinke at whose feet I had played, who had visited my sickbed and understood me when my parents did not, of Olga and our meetings and activities in her later years and the closeness between us. I remembered her bearing, the sound of her voice, the clear gaze of her green eyes.

I went back into the kitchen, made tea, filled the Thermos and took it with me to the dining table. It was afternoon; the sun was shining outside and the birds were singing.

I took the first letter and read.

Part Three

How could you lie to me like that? Will you be back
before winter sets in, I asked, and you said yes – it was
our last night, we had made love, we were so close – if
the truth wasn't sacred to you then, when is it sacred to
you? Have you always lied to me? Do you see me as a
child whom you just fob off with any old story? Or too
stupid, as a woman, for your great manly thoughts? Did
you want to spare me? It was yourself you spared, not me.
If you had told the truth, I would have told you the truth.
You did it in Karelia, so you can do anything? You were
lucky in Karelia. You've always been lucky, all your life.
It's gone to your head, and driven you out of your mind.

Two people have left your expedition. You had lied
to them, too. Did you want to be like Amundsen? Only
announce the great goal when there was no going back,
only victory or defeat? Amundsen wanted to beat Scott –
whom do you want to beat? Who apart from you is even
interested in Nordaustlandet and the Passage and the Pole?
Better in the bloom of life to be snatched away – you said it
had nothing to do with the expedition. That too was a lie.
You want to become a hero by perishing. So go! – No, I

don't wish such a terrible thing. But don't think that you will perish a hero up there. Heroes die for a great cause. You are dying for nothing. No daring struggle and no serving humanity. You're just freezing to death.

How can you do this? Throw me away, our love, our life, for an empty gesture? I know you aren't suited to an ordinary, bourgeois life; I have never asked it of you. But we had a life together, a life with interruptions, the kind a man and a woman have to endure when she stays at home and he has to go far away, as a soldier or explorer or captain. It was *our* life. Even though we yearned for each other when you were away, seized by wanderlust, when you were with me we were happy. It was an uneven happiness, but a true happiness. Our happiness. Does it matter less than the gesture with which you want to let yourself be snatched away in the bloom of life? What sort of asinine poem is that, anyway – *in the bloom of life to be snatched away* – nothing and no one is snatching you away! – *in the struggle to serve humanity* – humanity begins with humans, with you and me.

Again and again I allowed myself to be charmed by you, by your sparkling eyes when you were making plans or recounting stories, when you were setting off or on your return. You were like a child dazzled by the world and by life. But children don't put themselves at risk. They go to extremes, but they don't go beyond them. It's part of their charm. Your charm, I see now, is a rotten charm.

You have lied to me – lied twofold. If you had told me what you were planning I would have fought you, I would have shouted, begged, wept, I would have done all I could to dissuade you. If you had gone ahead none-theless, at least we would have had it out with each other.

Perhaps I would have understood you, seen a truth behind the empty gesture and the hollow words.

At first I was furious. Now I'm just sad. You have destroyed what was ours. As to why you did it, one reason is as bad as another: you were too cowardly for the truth, or too lazy for it, or else you gave no thought at all to the damage you were doing with your lies. I don't know how things between us can continue.

Herbert, my darling,

Are you holding this letter first? Don't read the other one.
When I heard that you were staying on the ice for the
winter, I was insane with worry. I reproached you. I was
hurt that you were putting your life and our happiness at
risk. But I don't want to reproach you. You want to test
yourself, your men, your equipment, you want to be ready
for your great feat. Or have you already set off on your
great feat? I want to believe in you. I am hoping with you
and praying for you. I hope you have the right clothes and
the right provisions and that you get along with your men
and retain your confidence. The newspaper says that you
left too late, that it will soon be winter. I now know that,
for you, it wasn't too late. You're not avoiding the winter,
you're seeking it.

It's myself I reproach, not you. For as long as I've
known you, you've always been daring, and since
Karelia you think that, for you, there are no limits. It
lights you up. I love your capacity for enthusiasm, for
spending yourself, for throwing yourself into things and

surmounting obstacles. I love your light. This is who you are; I cannot love you as you are and at the same time expect you to be sensible.

I am sensible. I should have talked to you and tried to dissuade you from spending the winter on the ice. Perhaps I would not have succeeded. But perhaps I would.

You will only read what I am writing to you once it's all over. I so wish my letters could accompany you, so you would always find one waiting for you: when the ship arrives, when you set off, when you set up camp. To me, it feels as if you're going to read my letter very soon and look troubled because I'm worried, and smile, because I love you for your radiance, and frown, because I would have tried to dissuade you from spending the winter on the ice. I have to force myself and tell myself that I am writing a letter that will lie unread for a long time. When you read it you'll be back in Tromsø; you've just telegraphed me and I'm not worried any more. If you know, telegraph me tomorrow or the day after to say when your ship will arrive in Hamburg and I'll be standing on the quay waiting for you. I miss you now, and I'll be missing you when you read this. Until you're back with me again.

My thoughts and my love go with you. I don't know how long you will still be on board ship, or when you'll arrive in Nordaustlandet.

I'm picturing it: snow, ice, mountains, rocks, glaciers, the snow piled up in drifts, the ice in towering floes, the glaciers full of fissures and above it all a night sky under which the pale sun appears only for a few hours on the horizon. When I picture it, I am afraid.

I am praying for you. But it's as if God cannot hear me, as if he's as far away as you, somewhere in the North, in the snow and ice. But perhaps it's good that he is where you are. God, protect my beloved.

Your Olga

21 September 1913

Dear Herbert, who is my first thought on waking and last thought before I go to sleep,

Today is Sunday, the church service and the organ playing are finished, and the school does not demand that I think about the children instead of you. We've been having sunny, warm summer days, but autumn is in the air today, and looking up into the trees I see the first yellow leaves. I can't think of the weather without thinking of you. May God give you mild weather.

School started again three weeks ago. As always, for the first week the children were still mentally on holiday; they couldn't sit still, and in the breaks they ran about and scuffled like young pups. Some of them were probably wishing they were back helping with the harvest, where I'd seen them slaving and sweating away. In the second week they were calm and quiet; that too is always the same, as if they've given up. This past week they've woken up again and have been joining in since then. Every term I worry in the second week that the children will stay calm and quiet. But every term the third week comes and saves us.

217

Fortunately, the schools inspector didn't visit until the third week. He watched sternly, and when he tried to conduct the children's singing at the end, they didn't make a sound until he let his monocle drop from his eye and sang loudly along with them. He was nice to me. He said that when I was transferred to Gumbinnen district, they'd been worried about me. There had been rumours, and while the management didn't concern itself with rumours, it did have to identify and avert any risks. Well now, whatever had happened, my lessons were good, and he was glad to have me as one of the district's teachers. What rumours, I wanted to know. Let's forget it, he said, there's nothing in your file.

All I knew back then was that Viktoria had spoken ill of me to the pastor. She must have done the same with all her girlfriends' fathers who were aristocrats or in the military or who ran the province as senior government officials. I still don't understand Viktoria. I don't understand why she pretended to be out when I called. In the end I waylaid her, and she actually ran away from me, down the street, and ducked behind the fence near the school. I knew where she was, I spoke to her, but she didn't answer, didn't come out from behind the fence, and I didn't want to drag her out. Perhaps I should have.

Why, Herbert? Because I'm no longer the poor orphan, grateful for the crumbs that fall from her table? Because I've studied? There are also those on the schools board – not the inspector, but others – who intimate to me that I shouldn't think I'm special just because I've studied; I'm merely a teacher. When – to commemorate your lecture there – I went to another lecture at the Tilsit Patriotic Society, about the preparations for the 1916 Olympic Games in Berlin, and tried to ask a question, I was ignored until I stood up, only to be told that we were out of time. Isn't it enough that I can't vote? That I earn less than a male teacher? That I can't be the headmistress of a school? Isn't it enough that they discriminate against us – do they have to humiliate us as well?

I've never spoken to you about these things, not even about Viktoria. I was too proud. And I was afraid of what you would say. I know it made you uneasy that I went to the training college and became a teacher. But what was I supposed to become? And could I have been your helpmeet during your preparations if I'd become a maid, or gone to work at the factory? How lovely it was last autumn, when you were writing your lecture and your letters and reading them out to me, and we would talk about them! You would sit at one end of the table and I at the other, knitting, or sewing, or sticking labels on the jam we made – do you remember?

Do you yearn for our quiet room?

When you return from the cold, will you find it so lovely and cosy here that you won't be plagued by wanderlust any more? Come home, my darling, come home.

Your Olga

19 October 1913

Once again I am with you, Herbert. But how could it be otherwise – you were with me all afternoon, making jam.

Yesterday I took the train to Mehlauken and picked seven pounds of raspberries in the forest. I could have picked a great deal more if the rain hadn't set in and refused to stop. A cold autumn rain that pelted down on the shed roof all night and all day today. It's quiet now. It's hot in the kitchen; I've opened the door to let in the fresh air.

Do you remember? How I dipped the sugar into cold water, dissolved it in the big pot over a low flame and let it seethe until it went clear? How I added the raspberries and boiled and stirred them until I had thick raspberry juice? You watched, wide-eyed. The jam was terribly sweet last year, so I used less sugar this time. Seven pounds of raspberries and eight pounds of sugar – I filled twenty-two jars! I would have loved to let you sulphur the jars and lids again. Remember? You held the thread of sulphur with the tongs, turning one glass after another upside down and sulphuring it; I filled them with raspberry juice, poured a teaspoon of rubbing alcohol on top, then we put the sulphured lids on the jars and covered them with greaseproof paper. Without you, I had to be as quick and accurate as a machine. I managed it, but I missed you. I miss you in everything we did together that I am now doing alone. And in everything I do alone that we haven't yet done together, but I know we could.

The only good thing about our separation is that I can write and tell you how much I miss you. When we're together and I tell you how much I've missed you or am going to miss you, you frown and don't like to hear it. You think I want to hold you back and forbid you to leave. I'm not holding you back. I know you have to leave. I just miss you.

I'm happy about the jam I made today, though. The jars will sweeten the winter for me. And when I'm spreading the jam from the last of the jars on my bread, you'll be here again.

Your Olga

Advent Sunday 1913

November was terrible. Eik caught diphtheria, which the doctor didn't recognize at first. It started with fatigue and a sore throat; then Eik complained of stomach ache and threw up. Nothing serious, we thought, even when he developed a slight fever; children just shouldn't play outdoors on cold, damp autumn days as if it were still summer. But the fever worsened, and the doctor came. An old man, calm and friendly; lives in Schmalleningken, covers the villages, has brought all the children into the world and closed the eyes of all the dead. He means well. The fact that his hearing and eyesight aren't good hadn't bothered anyone before. His sense of smell isn't good, either; he didn't smell the rotten, sickly-sweet odour emanating from Eik's mouth, and although I could smell it, I didn't yet know that it indicated diphtheria.

How Eik suffered! He coughed, barking, first at night, then during the day as well, couldn't swallow, could hardly speak, could hardly breathe. His body burning up; the pain, the fear of choking to death – no child should have to suffer like that, and I wished that I could suffer in his place. Every day after school I rushed over there and made compresses for his throat and calves, cooled his face, made him drink egg yolk in red wine, echinacea and garlic tea, feeling so powerless the whole time, so helpless. It was as if God weren't hearing my prayers, as if he were a very long way away, as if I had prayed to him to be with you instead of with Eik, to protect the man I love instead of the child. When I wasn't watching over Eik I was weeping, and when I fell asleep I woke again straight away.

I had the feeling the doctor was missing something, and it drove me into Tilsit, to the library. I found a report about diphtheria, and when I pointed out the symptoms to the doctor he wasn't offended; he understood. It was very late: Eik should really have been given the antitoxin within three days of the onset of disease. But it wasn't too late, and since he's been given it things have improved. He's weak, and will remain so for a long time; he's not allowed to exert himself, or even sit up. But what happiness to be nursing him back to health rather than in the fear that he was getting more and more sick.

Today is the first day I've been able to leave Eik on his own. The first day I'm able to think about school again and about repairing the roof, and the coal for the winter that still hasn't arrived. I think about you, but I've thought about you every day. You should have been with me at Eik's bedside. You don't understand that, I know, and my head tells me I can't reproach you, but my heart is full of accusation.

I see you in my mind's eye, the way you would look at me when you listened to me. Unsure what it is I want from you, resentful because you haven't done anything deserving of accusation, guilty because you don't love me as I love you, hoping everything will soon be fine again. You are a child, Herbert.

Your Olga

My dear Herbert,

Perhaps if you hadn't put your life at risk I would never have told you. But it has made possible what was previously impossible, and the unsayable can be said.

Eik is your child. I thought that surely you would realize the first time you saw him, or if not the first time then the second or third. I thought that surely you would recognize your own flesh and blood. He is so like you in so many ways: his build, his decisiveness and fearlessness, the artless egotism with which he hurts others without meaning to hurt them – he simply doesn't see them. When he's excited about something, when he succeeds in doing something, he lights up just like you.

I knew I was pregnant a few weeks after you left for German South-West Africa. That my body had been blessed – that was what I felt then, even though I didn't know how I was going to cope with the situation. That is what I feel now, too: Eik is a blessing in my life.

I was lucky. Sanne is the sister of a friend from teacher training college. She helped me with the birth, she reported

Eik as a foundling and took him in, and the authorities are glad he's provided for. I give her what I can. She isn't doing it for money. We've become friends. She isn't raising Eik as her own child; I didn't want that. She tells him that she found him, that she liked him and kept him. He knows that she loves him, and he knows that I love him – Sanne's friend, a sort of auntie.

I was very afraid. Afraid that people would see I was pregnant. That the contractions would start while I was in the middle of moving here. That I would give birth before Sanne managed to get to me. That I would scream during the birth.

But all went well. I made myself the right clothes, sent the neighbour's boy to fetch Sanne at the right moment, and didn't scream. Eik entered the world one day after I arrived here.

Why didn't I tell you? I would have, if you had recognized him. If not as your son, then as my happiness. But you didn't see him, and so he is mine and mine alone. All I want is for you to know, when you come back, who I am. I am not just the woman you know, the woman who loves you. I am Eik's mother.

Sometimes I wake and it feels as if you won't come back. Sometimes I wake and it feels as if you'll come back and I won't be alive any more. The games fear plays with us! But if that happens, you must help Sanne. Without demands, without expectations, at best without words.

In spite of everything, I am still

Your Olga

Christmas 1913

Everything is white. It already was when I wrote my last letter, but I couldn't appreciate it then, when I was writing. And it wasn't as beautiful then as it is today. It started snowing yesterday morning and only stopped early today. It was still light as I walked to church yesterday for one last rehearsal with the choir before Christmas vespers, but the snow was falling so thickly that I had difficulty finding the path. On the way back it was dark, and I walked right past my house. I soon found it again – it's not as if there are a lot of houses here – but for a moment I was completely lost in the darkness, the snow and the cold. Like you.

Now the sky is blue, and the sun is shining, and the snow is glittering. After the service I went to see Eik, but I had to come back soon afterwards. My neighbour had lent me a horse and sledge – I couldn't have got through otherwise – and he needed both himself that afternoon. I would have liked to stay longer. I would also have liked to drive the sledge for longer over the snow. Now I'm sitting at the table looking out at the wide field. The whiteness is blinding. A buzzard is circling in the sky. From time to time it plunges down and finds the mouse beneath the snow; it's a mystery to me how. I wonder whether it's the buzzard we saw on our last picnic?

Where are you, my love? On your ship, in the pack ice? In a hut? I read that fishermen and hunters and explorers had built huts on the islands of the Spitsbergen archipelago. In an igloo? I've read about the cosy dwellings that Eskimos build out of snow and ice, and I hope you can do what they can. Both of us are without a Christmas tree this year: you don't have one, so I didn't want one, either. But you'll have a light, a candle or a lamp. I lit the fat red candle for you that we bought last year, which will last a long time. Next Christmas we'll light it again together.

Three years ago today you asked me if I would marry you, and you didn't understand why I said no. It wasn't just that I would have lost my job, and not knowing what I would do without it when you're away on your constant travels. Nor was it just the fear that you would come to resent me one day if your parents cut you off and disinherited you. Or the fear of what we would live on when your aunt's inheritance was used up. It was Eik. We couldn't have acknowledged that we were his parents without there being a scandal and a court case and prison.

We wouldn't have been able to bring him to live with us as a foster child, either; they don't just transfer children from one foster family to another without good reason. So all that would have remained would have been for you and me to live together as man and wife, with him, our child, separated from us. It would be so wrong that I can't do it.

And there's something else. As a child, I so longed for a family in which I was loved, one that strengthened me and helped me. I didn't have that; I had to do everything alone. I had Eik alone, too, and I've looked after him alone.

I managed all of this, and I'm proud of it. It's too late for me to learn how to live together the way you men expect. I will not adapt myself, will not subordinate myself. Could you learn to live with that? Would you want to?

I dream about it sometimes. That you come back and ask me all the things you never asked me: how I would like to live, whether I would rather do something other than teach children who don't want to be taught, and what that might be, what I would like to see of the world, where I would like to travel and where I'd like to live, how you could help me with all that. Even in Prussia women can study at university; I wouldn't have to go to Zurich any more, just to Berlin.

Sending you love from my dreams,

Your Olga

New Year 1914

My love,

I was at Sanne's farm for New Year's Eve, spent the night there, and walked home early this morning. Between Christmas and New Year it had got warmer, the snow had melted a bit, then it got colder again, the snow froze, and this morning the ice crystals sparkled in the sun more brightly and beautifully than I have ever seen. If only you could have seen them with me!

Yesterday evening Eik was as lively and cheerful as before his illness. Sanne's elder children were allowed to stay up until midnight; Eik had to go to bed with the little ones after the festive dinner, and complained bitterly. But scarcely had he got into bed than he was asleep. I'm going to ask the doctor whether Eik still needs to convalesce. If he needs to, then he must, even if it's not easy to calm him down.

I've made a lot of plans for the new year. I want a piano, and I want to practise all the Beethoven sonatas. I want a bicycle, to get to Eik more quickly and easily and to be able to go to a concert or lecture in Tilsit even if there are no trains after it finishes. For both of these I need money, even if I buy them second-hand, and Sanne and I are planning to make jam that she'll sell on the market in Tilsit. I want to keep chickens and a goat. I've always shuddered at the thought of goat's milk, I don't know why; I tried it recently for the first time and it was delicious. I want to read Dante's *Divine Comedy*.

I want to talk to you about lots of things. Maybe I'm wrong. Maybe a lawyer would tell us we can acknowledge Eik as our child and bring him to live with us and not have to go to prison for all sorts of crimes. Maybe we can marry after all. If I lose my job, I can write a book for you about your expedition; you just have to tell me all about it. The book's success will mean we'll be able to manage even after your aunt's inheritance runs out. Or maybe your parents will show some understanding after all. What are they going to do with the estate if they don't give it to you?

Oh, Herbert: yesterday a lively and cheerful Eik at the end of the old year, today the radiant morning at the start of the new – I am filled with hope. Perhaps 1914 will be our year!

Your Olga

2 January 1914

Today the Tilsit newspaper reports that your ship is frozen in pack ice. That it set you down with three companions, but couldn't pick you up again at the agreed rendezvous. The captain left the ship and, with great difficulty, managed to reach a settlement.

Where are you, my love? Are you spending the winter in a hut? Or did you return to the ship and are spending the winter there? Or have you set out for a settlement, too – will I read about you in the newspaper in the coming days, as I did today about the captain? He was completely exhausted and frozen half to death – I've read that your toes freeze and fall off first, but that you can still walk and run and dance without toes, and if you run a little less and spend more time here with me that's no bad thing, and however exhausted you are I'll get you well again. We haven't danced together often, only once in fact, when there was a church fête in Nidden, and at first you didn't want to, but then you danced with me so gaily, it couldn't have been more gay. It was a *Ländler*, I'd like to dance waltzes with you, and – because I don't know how and maybe you don't either – take classes with a dancing master.

There are so many things I would like to do with you.

232

Dance, go skating, go sledging, go mushrooming, look for bilberries, read to and be read to by you, sleep and wake with you, travel with you, in trains and carriages and hotels, like rich people. I would not like to travel with you to the Arctic.

But I would like to be with you now, even if it were bitterly cold on the ship or in the hut or perhaps in a tent or a cave. We would keep each other warm.

Your Olga

17 February 1914

My love,

A German rescue team set off to search for all of you yesterday. A Norwegian team headed out in January, right after the captain appeared; it had to turn back without success because of adverse weather conditions. The German rescue team is confident. But you were confident, too, and Germans are always confident, and Norwegians know their way around best up there. Often I can't sleep for worry.

And your father's visit has made the worry even worse. Yes, you read that right: your father came here. He was waiting for me today at the school; I recognized him immediately, although it's been many years. He's grown old and walks with a stick; his hair is white and his face covered in age spots. But he was standing very upright in the dirty snow outside the school, in a fur coat and lace-up boots; he walks very upright, though it's a visible effort for him; his voice is strong, and the stick is topped with a silver knob.

He wanted to know what I knew about your plans. Like me, he and your mother had expected you to return before winter, and now they were wondering whether you had lied to them and had intended all along to spend the winter in Nordaustlandet, or whether you had quite different objectives – the North-East Passage, the North Pole – that they didn't know about. Your father wants to support another rescue expedition that would set out in March, when the weather is better and they can be more certain of success. Where should the rescue expedition look?

We walked through the slush in the street and then along the path that leads around the school to my apartment, and your father's car followed us, even though it's only a few metres. In my apartment he looked around as if expecting hideous poverty, and realized to his astonishment how pleasant it is in my home. He didn't take off his coat, but he sat down, I made tea and told him what little I knew. He listened to me, and at the end he sat there and said nothing, just nodded a couple of times.

Then he stood. Your father was never patronizing towards me, as your mother and Viktoria in particular could be, just distant. He politely demanded respect, and he treated me in the same way, young as I was: with politeness and respect. I think that sometimes, when he was bothered by the familiarity between you and me, he was cold, but he was always polite. No one could insist more genteelly on the gulf between the lord of the manor and the petite bourgeoise, or whatever it is I am.

He stood before me and raised his head, and I saw that he was weeping. Tears rolled down his cheeks; he shut his eyes tight and pressed his lips together, and his shoulders twitched. 'I'm sorry,' he kept repeating, 'I'm sorry.' I went over to him and wanted to hug him, as I hug my pupils, even the big boys, but he shook his head and left. I followed him to the corner of the street and watched him get into the car and watched the car drive away.

'I'm sorry' – I can still hear him; it sounds terrible, as if he were speaking of your death, as one mourner to another. But that can't be right; he believes you'll be rescued and is supporting an expedition. If not that, what was it? What is he sorry for? And why did he come? I would have written and told him what I knew if he had asked me in a letter.

So I'm confused, and the confusion intensifies the worry. If you're on the way to the nearest settlement, keep going. And if you have to stay in a hut, keep holding on until you can leave or rescue arrives.

I keep on holding you with love,

Your Olga

8 March 1914

It's spring! I spent the night at Sanne's and walked across the fields first thing in the morning. If you look closely at the bushes and trees you can hardly see the green buds. But when the sun had risen and the sky brightened and the birds were clamouring, a tinge of green lay over the grey-brown forest. There are yellow buds on the forsythias beside the church door.

The spring gives me courage. When it was winter here, I envisioned you in winter, too. Now it feels as if spring must have come to you, too, as if the snow and ice must be melting and the rocks peeping through and the little streams flowing. Do you remember how you asked me what grows in the icy wastes? Nothing grows in the icy wastes, but on Nordaustlandet there is the tundra, and in spring it will be green here and there, and perhaps one or two little flowers will bloom. I know everything is later with you than it is here. But when the time comes and you see the first blossom – will you think of me? Yes, you will, I know it.

What is longing? Sometimes it's like an object that can't be ignored, can't be moved, that often blocks the way, but that belongs in the room and to which I have grown accustomed. And then it suddenly hits me like a blow that makes me want to scream.

I don't want to pester you; how could I? You will come when you come. But I won't let you go again.

Your Olga

15 March 1914

My husband,

Because that is what you are, whether state and church have
married us or not. You are the father of my child, you are
my husband.

I was in Tilsit with Eik, and as we were passing the Wilhelm
Nagelhort photographic studio I couldn't resist: I went in and
had our photograph taken. Here is the picture. We could have
let ourselves be photographed against a backdrop; there was
one screen with the High Dune, one with an oak forest and
one with medieval walls. But I didn't want that. I just wanted
us in the photograph, me on the chair and Eik beside me.
He found it all a bit uncanny: the screens, the props, which
included a lion skin with a lion's head, a small cannon, and
a rocking horse with real horse skin and a leather bridle; the
big photographic apparatus on its spindly legs and Wilhelm
Nagelhort under the black cloth. And the magnesium light!
We had prepared Eik, had told him it would blind him, but it
still came as a shock and he jumped up and stood there stiff as
a poker. He'd been leaning against me until then; I liked that.

But he isn't keen on leaning and cuddling any more. He's

239

turning into a proper boy. He reminds me of you. His eyes are as blue and clear as yours. He's going to be taller than you, but just as sturdy and strong. He doesn't run. But he too wants to be somewhere that isn't where he is, he just doesn't know where.

Would others see you in him? I do. It makes me happy. It makes me sad. If only you were here and I could say to you: see how Eik stamps his foot defiantly, like you, and you would laugh and reply that my defiance was in my chin, and that Eik has my chin. We would argue about which of us was more defiant, and Eik wouldn't realize that our argument wasn't serious and would come up to us, worried, wanting to reconcile us, and we would all hug each other, all three of us.

Another expedition has set off to Nordaustlandet. They say Count Zeppelin is financing it. Should all these expeditions make me take heart? They make me afraid.

I am yours, as you are mine,

Olga

5 April 1914

Herbert, my dearest,

Today is Palm Sunday, we sang Bach's choral motet from *King of Heaven, Be Thou Welcome,* and I would have liked to have had a big choir and a big orchestra. But there are some strong voices in my choir, and the organ stood in for the orchestra. I directed, played and sang, and the pastor, who never usually says anything, praised me.

It's turned cold; the newspaper writes that we haven't had such a cold April since 1848, when meteorological records began. It's killed off the tree blossom, and poor families don't know where they're supposed to find money for coal. I have a warm stove and hot tea and a guilty conscience, because I'm fine. I hope you're being spared this dreadful weather.

I just got up and went to the cupboard, and behind my reserves of sugar and honey I found your notebooks. As if you had wanted to hide them from me. Or did you want to find a place for them where they wouldn't bother me? Your notes don't bother me!

No, that's not true. I read them and they made me cross. The allure of distant lands, the expanses of the desert and the Arctic, your longing for somewhere and nowhere, your colonial fantasies – such castles in the air! I know you're not alone in building them. Not a week goes by when I don't read about Germany's future on the high seas and in Africa and Asia, about the value of our colonies, about the strength of our navy and our army, about Germany's greatness, as if we had outgrown our country the way one outgrows a robe and needed a bigger one.

For a long time your dreams were more honest than that. You loved emptiness, the emptiness of the desert and – you didn't know it yet, but it enticed you – the emptiness of the Arctic. Later you talked about plantations, factories and mines in the desert, and about the North-East Passage – you disguised your love of emptiness the way politicians and newspapers disguise their love of emptiness with economic and military goals. It's not about the goals. They're puffed-up nonsense, just as Germany's greatness is puffed-up nonsense. Sometimes I read and hear that there will be war soon. In a war, nothing will be left of the colonies, nothing, and no one will let Germany keep the big robe it doesn't actually need.

The French and the English and the Russians had their fatherlands early on; for a long time, the Germans had theirs only as a fantasy, not on earth but in heaven – Heine writes about it. On earth they were divided, riven with strife. By the time Bismarck finally created their fatherland for them, they had grown accustomed to fantasizing. They can't stop. They go on fantasizing; now it's about Germany's greatness and its triumphs on the seas and on distant continents and about economic and military marvels. They're empty fantasies, and it's the emptiness that you actually love and seek. You write about devotion to the great cause, but you mean melting away into emptiness, into nothingness. I fear the nothingness into which you want to melt away. It's greater than the fear you will meet with an accident. I didn't take what you wrote seriously back then. I thought it strange, but that didn't matter, because you were near me. Now you are far away. In your notebooks I meet you as a stranger, and I see that you were already a stranger to me then.

I hold you tight, in desperation,

Your Olga

6 April 1914

Dearest,

Everything I wrote yesterday is true, and yet . . .

I love your radiance, your determination, your persistence. Whenever you encounter misfortune, you brush it off – like a dog coming out of the water and shaking himself to make the drops fly away. You were never able to comfort me when I was sad; you would stand beside me in my sorrow like a helpless child. After a while, though, you would think of a way to draw me out of my sorrow with some mad or silly thing. Even when we were young – do you remember how I despaired when my grandmother had hidden my books, and you dyed your hair with shoe polish and drew on a moustache to play the robber at Grandmother's house and fetch the books? And the time we sat beside the Neman, and I was sad, because I couldn't get my favourite pupil into high school in Tilsit, until you climbed the poplar tree, dizzyingly high, to prove to me that anyone who really wants to reach the top can get there. You have a wild imagination and a wild longing and you deserved a better focus for both than our age has to offer.

Perhaps you will still find it.

And along with the wildness you have another side that I love no less. Perhaps I love it even more. Your devotion. I never had to ask you, you never had to reassure me: I know – you never had another woman, not in the brothels of Berlin like other officers, and not on your travels. Whenever you came back to me, after a short time or a long one, you asked me whether I still cared for you, still loved you, still wanted you, not because you'd done something that might have cost you my love, but because my love for you is a miracle you can scarcely believe. Whenever you said goodbye, you said, 'Don't forget me,' as if I could ever forget you, and for a long time I didn't understand that you simply wanted the same fixed place in my heart that I have in yours. You're a little timid, even if you don't admit it to yourself, but you're not a timid lover, you're passionate, and at the same time tender and gentle. You've cultivated your own expectations of your life, as I have of mine. But the realm of love is something we created together, and here there is nothing that you hold back from me or I from you. Here you are as attached to me as I am to you. Oh, my dearest. When you're with me, it's easy for me to accept your two sides. Like when you're standing beside me singing the 'Deutschlandlied' and at first it's Deutschland that's *über alles* for you, and then you're filled with enthusiasm for German women and German loyalty and you smile at me and take my hand.

Your Olga

11 April 1914

Herbert, my love,

The newspaper is full of you again. A few days ago, the Norwegians from your expedition arrived at the settlement the captain also reached at the end of last year. They had no news of you; they had spent the winter on board ship in the pack ice, and left it in the spring.

At least they survived the winter, and the paper says that what was possible on board ship is also possible in a hut, or even in a well-situated, well-secured tent. Perhaps you and your people have also returned to the ship by now. There's hope that, in the coming months, you too will turn up at the settlement, or that one of the expeditions currently underway will find you.

On 12 May it will be four years since you gave your lecture to the Tilsit Patriotic Society for Geography and History about Germany's mission in the Arctic. The society has planned an event on that day, commemorating your lecture. They hoped to be able not just to pay tribute to you but to welcome you as well; at present, things are looking auspicious for your rescue.

No, I'm not going to start on again about your longing for the great expanse. But there is one thing that bothers me. I hardly ever travel any further than Tilsit. The trip to Posen for the anniversary of our graduation from teacher training college was the longest trip I've made in years. I didn't tell you about the anniversary, because you're not interested, and I won't tell you about it now. It was at the start of the school holidays, so I was able to stay on in Posen for a day after the celebration. That evening, as I walked around the town – which I like – on my own, and the bells were ringing and the lights going on in the houses and shining from the windows, I felt homesick for my dilapidated village and my wretched apartment at the back of the school. I know, that sounds ridiculous, but listen. It's not that when I'm in my dilapidated village and my wretched apartment at the back of the school I am content. I often want to leave; I often want to go out into the world and see Paris and Rome and London, and the Alps and the ocean. I have wanderlust. And my wanderlust feels no different from my homesickness: a tugging in the stomach, my chest starts to feel tight, and my throat fills with tears that I cannot shed, but that stop me breathing freely.

Perhaps the longing to reach your destination has been consumed by your longing for nothingness and the great expanse. Just as Germans long for emptiness and, at the same time, for comfort. I have never insisted you reveal your thoughts and feelings to me. But when you come back, I don't want you to hide any more by saying you can't explain what you're feeling.

Come back soon!

Your Olga

13 May 1914

Dearest,

A month has passed since I last wrote to you. I lost faith.
For a long time, it felt as if by writing these letters to you I
was keeping you in the world and preserving and protecting
you. These past few weeks, I couldn't believe it any more.
When I sat at the table and wrote to you, no courage or
strength flowed into the letter, only ink.

Things are better again today. Yesterday the event in
Tilsit was held in your honour, and any day now another
expedition is setting out to rescue you. The speeches at the
event and the newspaper report were optimistic. The report
doesn't gloss over the criticism of your belated departure to
the Arctic, but it pays tribute to your strength of will and
initiative, and quotes a researcher who says the success of an
expedition is five per cent dependent on the equipment, five
per cent on timing, and ninety per cent on its leader. I can't
really envisage this, and I'd never heard of the researcher,
either. But I know that, as a leader, you won't fall short.

At the end of the event they sang 'Deutschland, Deutschland
über alles' again, like last time. As if Deutschland is going

to bring you back to me. Perhaps some brave, competent Norwegians will. It was all too loud. I thought of you, and in my thoughts it was completely silent all around you; the snow was falling quietly, covering everything with a white blanket. They frightened me, the silence and the blanket.

The day before the event, the schools board had invited me to a teachers' conference in Tilsit. They talked about you there, too, and you were praised and damned and everything in between. I defended you; it did me good. The schools inspector who visited me in September came as well; he offered me his arm and was friendly in a paternal way, as if he knew about you and me and wanted to express his sympathy. Is it possible he knows about us?

It was the first teachers' conference I'd attended. I learned that teachers have very different ways of dealing with parents who want to put their children to work in the fields instead of sending them to school. I've always said no. From now on, we were asked to be generous in granting their wish. A young colleague sitting beside me said, 'So that's it, then.' We'd been chatting earlier, and had got along, and I asked him what he meant by 'that's it'. War, he said: we were to prepare the children to take their fathers' place.

I met a lot of young colleagues; there are more of us than we realized, and we want to go on meeting privately. I'm also going to get more involved with the association of women elementary schoolteachers. I don't want my life to be limited by the boundary of my village any longer.

I've been saving, and soon I'll have enough money to buy myself either a second-hand bicycle or a second-hand piano. I have to decide. It's going to be the bicycle; I want to get out of my village, and although I don't have a piano, I do at least have the organ.

This is what my life is like these days. I think of you; not five minutes go by without me thinking of you, there's not an evening when my last thought isn't of you, or a morning when it isn't my first. May my thoughts bear you up!

Your Olga

16 June 1914

Oh, Herbert, my love,

May was not a good month. In May a German–
Norwegian expedition reached your ship and saved the two
Germans who had stuck it out on board. You and your
companions were not on the ship, and the Germans had
no news of you. One expedition is still underway. They're
looking for you along the east coast of Nordaustlandet. The
newspaper says they should look for you on the west coast.
The paper also says you should have reached the settlement
by now. Wounds or frostbite might hold a group up, but if
one person were still able to set off, he would, and if none
of you were in a condition to do so and you were stuck in a
hut or a tent, searching for you was like searching for a needle
in a haystack. The paper mentions a Danish expedition that
survived two winters in Greenland. But it writes that Eskimos
helped the Danes, and there are no Eskimos and no Lapps
on Nordaustlandet.

When I've written to you about my life in my letters, it's
felt as if you were able to watch me, to be with me. From
far away, but I didn't sense the distance. Now I do. Will

what I'm writing still reach you? I feel closest to you when I write about you and your ship and your people and the expeditions to save you. When I tell you about the events of my everyday life, it drops into the gulf that has opened up between us.

I don't want that gulf to be there. I want you to stay with me. Eik is interested in expeditions. Sanne doesn't get the newspaper; he reads it at my house, and he read about you and asked me about the Eskimos and the Lapps. I met up with one male colleague and seven of the female colleagues I got to know at the teachers' conference. The other male colleagues preferred to meet without the women, and the other female colleagues were worried the meeting might annoy the schools board. We resolved never to talk about ourselves, only ever about classes and the children, and, this time, about how to persuade parents and pastor to send a child to high school or the girls' secondary school. I'd had more success with this than the others in recent years. In the end, we did talk about ourselves, after all. One of us wants to get married, but her fiancé doesn't earn enough; between the two of them they would earn enough, but if she got married she would have to leave the teaching profession. Incidentally, the male colleague who came has inherited a bicycle that he doesn't ride because it's a women's bicycle; he's offered to sell it to me for a good price. Sanne and I preserved jam and are going to sell it on the market in Tilsit next Sunday, as we planned on New Year's Eve. Sanne's husband has built me a henhouse, and I'm getting chicks next week and will soon have chickens, which was also one of my plans.

Do you remember, four years ago, after your lecture, how we heard the song of the nightingale? This summer I hear it every night. I like its fluttering and trilling, but I really love its long notes; they pierce my soul.

The summer is warm, and I would like to lie with you beside the Neman, or beside the sea, and bid the day farewell and welcome the night and look up at the sky; at first it's still light, then dark, and our gaze finds stars upon stars and loses itself in the depths of the sky. The nightingale sings of love and death; our love, our death.

When I asked you what attracted you to the Arctic, you couldn't give me an answer. Do you have one now? Either to the Arctic or to war, you said, and that friends of yours said war was coming soon. Old Mina says the same; she claims to have seen the four horsemen.

I often feel as if I can't stand it any more, that it's all too much, the love, fear, hope, despair, closeness and estrangement. Sometimes I'm so angry with you it almost rips me apart, and then I'm immediately consumed by my guilty conscience. Come, I keep calling out to you, come; but you don't hear me. Hear me – come!

Your Olga

1 July 1914

My dear Herbert,

June was a bad month, too. The last expedition that was
still looking for you has returned. They found no trace of
you, no message left in a cairn, as expeditions usually do, no
abandoned tent, no equipment left behind. Your ship is in
Spitsbergen again; the ice released it, and the men from the
expedition brought it back.

There will be no more rescue missions. On 28 June
a Serb murdered the heir to the Austrian throne and his
wife in Sarajevo. Many are saying that Austria will declare
war on Serbia; many fear that Russia will stand by Serbia.
Whatever happens – no one is going to raise the money and
the personnel for another expedition to the Arctic. You're
on your own.

When the newspaper reported on the return of the rescue
expedition, it speculated about your and your companions'
prospects. Your provisions, the provisions that previous
expeditions and fishermen and hunters have left behind in
huts and camps, could last a long time. But it said the idea
that all four of you had been wounded and had recovered

over the summer and would soon turn up again was too unlikely. One should never abandon belief or hope; people sometimes surpass themselves and are carried beyond their limits by miraculous powers. However, one should think with love of those to whom you have not returned, and probably never will.

No, I am not abandoning belief or hope, and I think with love of no one but you. Yes, you were sometimes distant from me in recent months. But you are no more distant now than you were before you returned from the last expedition, or any more distant than you were before you set off. I don't care what they write about you. You remain in my heart, and I hope with you and believe in you and love you and am

Your Olga

8 August 1914

My dearest,

Germany declared war on Russia, then on France, then
England declared war on Germany.

The 41st Regiment has marched out. I was with the
schoolchildren in Tilsit. There was music and flowers, men
waved their hats, young women let soldiers take them in
their arms and saw them off at the station, and the trains
were hung with slogans: 'An outing to Paris' and 'Off to
flog the Frog'.

Here in the village there's no enthusiasm. Every call-up is
a blow for farm and family. The few volunteers are young
people whose fathers treat them worse than slaves. One came
to bid me farewell; he was afraid of war, but he was more
afraid of his father.

War is a thing for city people, not farmers. And for
children. The small and weak are made to play the Serbs
and the English, then the others set upon them, shouting,
'Serbia must die' and 'May God punish England!' The fear
of a Russian invasion is also greater among farmers, who
are worried about their supplies, than among city dwellers,

who have fond memories of the Russian officers from the nearby Tauroggen garrison when they were guests in the Hôtel de Russie.

I can imagine what you would do. You wouldn't hesitate to report to your regiment. For one unthinking moment I was happy that you were safe on Nordaustlandet.

Your Olga

13 September 1914

My love,

Yesterday our soldiers beat the Russians. Their infantry and the Cossacks had been occupying Tilsit since 26 August, and everything was fine with them. Once, a troop of Cossacks turned up in our village, let the children admire them and the mayor serve them beer, and were soon gone again. The farmers had hidden their wives and daughters and maids in cellars and attics, but the Cossacks didn't ask for women.

I know there's no hope of your return. But I've been writing to you for a year now, and your not answering today is no different from your not answering before. Nothing has changed. I can't reach you, but I couldn't reach you before, either. I see you in my mind's eye: all bundled up, your face framed by the fur lining of your coat and hood, on skis, your hands in mittens resting on the sticks, straps over your shoulders, pulling a sledge. You've become this figure in the snow and ice, far away, white and cold, and even if I had you with me I don't know if I could warm you. You've been carried away from me. But you are not dead to me.

Sometimes I tell Eik about your travels. I read him the letters you wrote to me, I embellish them here and there, and in Eik's eyes you are a great adventurer. He remembers you, and is proud when I tell him he's as brave and strong as you. I ought to warn him. I don't want him to lose himself as you lost yourself. But I can't bring myself to do it. We sit together, I tell him stories, his eyes light up, and when I break off at a particularly exciting point he doesn't want to wait until the next day or the day after for the next instalment, he takes my hands and begs and pleads. These are moments of closeness.

Be safe, Herbert, wherever and however you are. I love you.

Your Olga

11 November 1914

My love,

News of the war is coming in every day, and when the news
is of victories, bells are rung and flags are waved. Two people
from the village have been killed, and when I hear the news
all I can think of are the sacrifices that every day of war and
every victory demands.

Today the paper has a report about the regiments of young
men who advanced on the French yesterday at Langemarck.
With the 'Deutschlandlied' on their lips, oblivious to enemy
fire, they stormed the hill and took the French position. The
flower of our youth fell in rich sheaves, it said, but our pride
in those young men consecrates the pain of their death.

I see you among them. I see you running, in a field-grey
uniform, the ridiculous spiked helmet with the field-grey
cover, the knapsack on your back and the rifle with the fixed
bayonet in your hand. The knapsack is grey, too, and so are
your face and hands, so are the grass and the trees, so is the
sky, everything is grey. You're going up a slope, you run and
fall and get up and keep running, and I don't know whether
you fall because you stumble or because you've been hit, and

whether you keep running because you're back on your feet or in spite of the fact you're already dead. There are others around you; they run too, they fall too, but they don't get back up and they don't keep running. Only you get up and keep running, but you don't reach the top, you stay on the slope, you run and run and you don't get there, not to the French position and not into the arms of Death.

I see you as if in a dream and know that it's a dream I will dream again and again, night after night, until you come again, until the war is over. I never dreamed of you in the Arctic; I tried to imagine you in ice and snow, but I never really could, not waking and not sleeping. I've sometimes dreamed that you were going away in a carriage or on a train or on a ship; you stand on the platform or on deck, you turn to me, but you don't wave, you just look, and you're further and further away, getting smaller and smaller. Dreams of farewell, from which I awaken sad and full of tenderness for that little chap getting smaller and smaller.

You won't sing when you run up the slope at night in my dream. No one will sing. Amidst all that killing and dying, there is silence.

Your Olga

Christmas 1914

My love,

Last year you said you'd be back by Christmas. This year,
the soldiers said they would. There's no relying on you men.

We have rain and mud for Christmas, no snow and no
blue sky. But the church was decorated, and I sang the
'Quem pastores laudavere' with the choir. I've never seen
the church so full; even old and sick people who would
normally have stayed at home wanted to be in the church
with the others this wartime Christmas Eve, the way sheep
huddle together when the wolf is howling outside. Four
families are now wearing black. When the pastor asked for
God's blessing on our guns, there was a shocked collective
intake of breath.

Sometimes I fantasize that you didn't stay on Nordaustlandet, but set off through the North-East Passage on skis, with
the sledge, to explore where the sea voyage might succeed
in summer. You made it to northern Siberia, were taken
in by natives during the winter and spring, and in summer,
when you tried to travel to Berlin via Moscow and first
encountered Russian officials, you found out that we were

at war and fled back to the natives, who aren't interested in war and peace, before you could be interned. That's where you are, and that's why you can't write to me. But you're alive, and you'll hurry back to me as soon as the war is over.

All the things I planned to do this year! Sanne and I earned money with the jam, and I bought a bicycle. But the fox took the chickens, and that discouraged me from keeping a goat. It'll be the year after next at the earliest before I have enough for a piano; and Dante's *Divine Comedy* starts with the Inferno, and I don't want to read about torture and pain and death. I don't want to read at all; cheerful books make me as sad as sad ones.

My Siberian fantasy figure, my dream love and my nightmare, my mad, lost, frozen, fallen husband, inadequate father of my son, my hope against all reason, my beloved, I cannot, will not let you go. Be always mine, as I am always yours,

Olga

11 July 1915

Herbert,

The battles this summer were more terrible than anything
we knew of war before now. They aren't reporting the
number of dead, but a colleague is in contact with someone
in Sweden, and they say it's in the hundreds of thousands.
We see more and more women in black. We also see more
and more wounded. For some the war is over, and Sanne is
happy, because her husband is home again. He has lost his
arm, and she says, what do we need his arm for? She won't
accept that he's lost more than that; he doesn't talk about
the horrors of war, but they're etched on his face.

The war is wiping out my generation of men. The young
colleague who came to the meeting with my female colleagues, who inherited the woman's bicycle and sold it on
to me, has also been killed. I sometimes thought that if you
didn't come back perhaps I could be happy with him. We
didn't promise each other anything, we just looked at each
other, and perhaps I saw more in his eyes than was really
there. But it was enough to let me think my life wasn't yet
over. Work goes on, of course, the school and the church,

and new pupils come each year. But I am not only your widow, and his, I am the widow of a generation.

You belong to the generation that is being wiped out, and I am beginning to grasp that you are dead. You're not just far away, unreachable. You really are dead, and if to me you are present, you are a figment of my memory and my longing. You are always present to me, still, and so I always have to tell myself that you are dead. I have to learn to live with this reality.

To learn not to write to you about the summer; about June, which was too hot, and July, which was too cool, about the Russian prisoners who are working on the farms and sometimes take the farmer's place not only on the farm and in the stable; about the children, who can see that the world is out of joint, that victory does not bring peace, that the Grim Reaper is like a godfather who makes himself at home in our families, and that fatherland, hero's death, honour and loyalty are just words. I have to learn not to tell you about my life. I'd been doing so less and less, anyway. Perhaps not me but something in me began to understand long ago that you are dead.

Olga

9 October 1915

Grandmother died a few days ago. She was ill, and I had offered to care for her here. But she wanted to die in her own bed. Or not have me around. She raised me, but she never took me to her heart. As if I were a disappointment, or a reminder of something unpleasant.

When I got there, she was already dead. She was lying in an open coffin in the cold church. I fetched a woollen blanket and pulled up a chair and sat down beside her. When it got dark, I lit a candle.

They hadn't closed her eyes and mouth in time. Her eyes weren't just open, they had seen the face of Death and were bulging with fear and terror, and her mouth had bared its toothless gums in a scream. It was completely silent in the church, and I could hear that scream until I put the lid on the coffin.

But Grandmother was still beside me, and I could sense her rejection, as I have always sensed it. Sometimes she would hit me, and she would often shout at me. But even when she wasn't doing any of that and didn't even speak to me harshly, her rejection hung in the air like a smell. I sat in the church and I could smell it again, that familiar, hated odour.

I used to wonder where this rejection came from, tried hard to do everything to please Grandmother, was hurt because nothing I ever did for her was right, and outraged when she punished me even though I had done nothing wrong. Now I was just sad. I thought of Eik. How nice it could have been for Grandmother to watch the young me grow up, how nice for me to have had an older woman to guide me. I would have liked to love her, if she had let herself be loved. And what happiness it would have been to have been loved myself!

'What happiness, ye gods, to love,' writes Goethe, setting it above being loved. Only someone who has the security of being loved can write this. I didn't have that security, ever.

Sometimes I felt sorry for myself, because I grew up without love, and even with you I could only live my love after a fashion. Now I think of the thousands of fallen soldiers, their unlived lives and unlived loves, and it drives away my self-pity. The sadness remains.

I sat beside the coffin and started crying and couldn't stop. Everything that should have been but never was between Grandmother and me and you and me and the soldiers and their wives and children – how am I to bear it? What is there left for me to take pleasure in? You died again that night, for the umpteenth time. Never had things seemed so empty in the light of your death.

After a while I got up and walked around the church. I sat at the organ I had practised and played on so often, and in the patron's box where I used to study and knit, and where we loved each other. I sat and cried, the memories hurt, and

267

yet I couldn't stop; I summoned up memory after memory and felt you beside me and missed you beside me.

When it grew light outside, I left. I walked across the fields to our spot at the edge of the forest. Nothing had changed. I stood and looked out, waiting for something, but I didn't know what; I saw the sun come up, illuminating first the treetops, then the trees, then the field. It was a wonderful sight.

Your – don't ask me how, but still your –

Olga

31 December 1915

My dearest, this is the last letter I shall write to you. I am saying goodbye to you. I am starting the new year without you. I don't want to have you around me, within me, any more.

You are dead, you have been dead for a long time, and I still talk to you, and when I do I see and hear you before me. You don't answer, but you laugh or grumble discontentedly or murmur in agreement. You are there. I've heard of phantom pains felt by soldiers who've lost an arm or a leg. It's gone, the arm or leg, but it hurts as if it's still there. You're gone, but you hurt as if you were still there.

If I can love you, even though you're dead, the way I loved you when you were alive – were you always a phantom? Did I always love only an image I created of you? An image for which it doesn't matter whether you're still alive, or dead?

I don't want to banish you from my life. You should still have a place in my heart, a shrine that is yours, only yours, before which I sometimes pause and think of you. But I have to be able to close the shrine and turn away from it. Otherwise it hurts too much.

Do you remember the first time we made love? We wanted to go for a walk, but we only got as far as our spot at the edge of the forest where we used to meet and talk and study, and where we realized that we belonged together. We stopped and put our arms around each other and lay down in the grass, and it was all so natural, and it was all so surprising. We were inconceivably happy. Then evening came; one of your bosses, a friend of your father's, was visiting your estate, and you had to go. I watched you leave; you turned and looked back at me. Then you were gone.

Go, my darling, look back once more for my sake, but go.

Olga

27 July 1936

Eik. He'd written to me that he wanted to see the Olympic Games, and perhaps he'd been working in Italy long enough and it was time to live in Germany again. He spent the week with Sanne, came to me at the weekend and left for Berlin today. He will see the Olympic Games. He will stay in Germany. It was only when we were saying goodbye at the station in Tilsit that he told me he was in the NSDAP and was joining the SS. He leaned out of the train window and acted as if some small thing had just occurred to him that he quickly wanted to mention.

What cowards you men are! You didn't have the courage to tell me beforehand about your overwintering nonsense, and he didn't either, to talk to me about his political madness. You both knew that I would argue with you, and you couldn't bear the argument. Snow and ice, guns and war – you men feel up to those, but not to a woman's questions.

These last few years I've often wondered what you would make of it all. I don't get the impression that the Nazis have colonial or Arctic dreams; perhaps that would save you from them. But everything is too grand with them, and where things are too grand, castles in the air are never far away.

Perhaps you would want to teach them to dream of colonies and the Arctic.

I am bitter, towards Eik and towards you. He is bone of your bones and flesh of your flesh. He is as stupid as you, and as cowardly as you. He can also be as sweet as you. But sweetness cannot compete with stupidity and cowardice.

Olga

Another letter immediately after the last one – we've had that before, I know. But this letter doesn't retract what was in the first, and you should read not just this one, but both of them.

Eik's announcement affected me so much that I had to write to you. My husband – his father. Eik is your son as he is mine, but he is more my son than yours, and Eik's letter was a shameful reminder to me of this. He wrote to me to justify himself while he was still on the train. I was the one who had taught him to delight in adventure, setting out to far-off places, life in the great expanse. That was what he had sought, and that was what he had found. Germany didn't need colonies. His *Lebensraum* was between the Neman and the Urals; for his generation, that was where adventure awaited, that was where he wanted to go, that was where he wanted to settle.

It's not you I reproach, but myself. He lived with me for a long time after the war, when he was at the high school, and I should have raised him better. I should have talked differently to him about you. Not as a hero, but as a melancholy knight who was not to be emulated, who missed

273

out on his own life by emulating others. You wanted to be Amundsen, and if not Amundsen, then Scott, instead of living your own life. Now Eik, too, wants to live a life that isn't for him. It won't end in ice and snow, but it will lead him into war.

It's strange. You don't feel any different to the way you did twenty years ago. You haven't aged in that time, either, but I have; and that might be enough, but isn't. Perhaps I've written to you because I'm lonely. Germany has become alien to me, and many people I used to be close to I no longer am, in the village, at church, in the choir. The old schools inspector shook his head worriedly when I refused to teach racial theory; the new one wants me out of the school.

I don't like going to church any more. I go for the organ and the choir. The pastor is a Nazi who drives all the joy of faith out of me. I don't believe in heaven and hell and life after death, anyway. So you are simply in my heart, and I send my love to you there.

Your Olga

15 October 1939

Herbert, dear,

I wrote to you three years ago. Soon after that I fell ill, and since then I haven't been able to hear. I was dismissed from teaching, went to the school for the deaf in Breslau, and now earn my living as a seamstress.

But that's not why I'm writing to you. I'm writing to you because of Eik.

He visits me every few months and is sweet and caring. If I weren't too proud, he would give me money and spare me the sewing. He didn't tell me what his work was, and I didn't ask, until his last visit, when he was too conceited to keep quiet about it. He works in the Reich Security Main Office; he started two years ago with the security police, is climbing the ladder, was promoted once last year and once this.

In the basement of the Reich Security Main Office they torture prisoners. I know it; everyone knows it. He said it had to be this way and I didn't understand it because I didn't understand the new times.

I understand the new times only too well. They are the old times, only now Germany is supposed to get even bigger and has even more enemies and has to triumph even more. And the screaming is even louder; I hear it even though I'm deaf.

I endured Eik's tirades about blood and soil. I cannot endure him sitting at a desk on the *bel étage* while people are being tortured in the basement. Does he visit the basement himself?

I wrote and told him I didn't want to see him any more. He came anyway; I said all I had to say, and he sat there obstinately in front of me. He reminded me of my schoolchildren, when I would tell them off for being mean, and they knew I was right but didn't want to stop their meanness. If it had been about something less important, his childish obstinacy would have moved me.

I have learned to live without you, and I will learn to live without Eik. It hurts.

Olga

1 April 1956

Herbert,

You should know that Eik is alive. He was released from captivity in Russia last year, one of the last ten thousand.

He wrote to me and visited me. He was self-pitying in the letter, and self-righteous when he visited. When I first saw him, his skinny frame, his emaciated face, his white hair, I felt sorry for him and took him in my arms. Then we spoke, and all he talked about was the injustice that had befallen him and Germany. He was a stranger to me, even stranger than before the war. He has a son and will soon have another child, his wife is pregnant, and I would like to get to know her, but he said I would only be allowed to do so if I didn't interfere in the children's upbringing and the affairs of the family. He could manage without me, he said, he had managed without me for fifteen years. And he didn't let anyone speak to him any more the way I used to speak to him.

He won't try to see me again. I won't try, either. I have remained lonely, and I have got used to it. I've become sort of friendly with the youngest child in one of the families I sew for. He's called Ferdinand; he reminds me a little of you and the young Eik, and I tell him about your adventures. But I make sure he doesn't think life is an adventure.

Sociable people live in the present, lonely people in the past. I often think of you, and our time together could not be more present if you and I had grown old together side by side. But it would be nice to reminisce together, you and me on a bench in front of the house: you think of something, I add something else, then I think of something and you carry on.

I often think of you while going about my daily chores as well. Then I talk to you; it's better than just talking to myself.

You are my partner, you became so early on and always have been. I get cross with you and argue with you, but that's why you are my partner, my husband, and I am glad that you are.

Your Olga

4 July 1971

Herbert, my dear, loyal husband,

I have read about artists who create something that doesn't bear their name, that no one recognizes as their work, that perhaps no one sees or hears. They find a stone basin eroded by a mountain stream and place an ornament of pebbles on the basin floor. They find a crack in the rock around which the wind blows, one that can fit a small glass pipe, or two or three, allowing the wind to whistle a note or a chord. They draw a pattern in the sand at low tide that's destroyed by the high tide a few hours later. Or is it not destroyed, but carried away?

A few weeks ago they blew up the water tower I could see from my balcony. It was as tall as a tall house, a slim outline rising up to the bulge of the container; it was made of brick and had a domed roof over the bulge and on top of that a little tower with another domed roof, and the roofs were made of slate. It was beautiful. It wasn't needed any more.

I'd read in the paper that they planned to blow it up, and when they started preparations I went along and spoke

279

to the demolition foreman. People don't refuse an old lady anything, so he explained to me how he was going to bring the tower down. The tower would not fall over, it would collapse in on itself and swirl up dust, but it wouldn't cause any damage. I went back again the next day, and again on the day of the explosion. The demolition foreman and workmen recognized me and were pleased that I was interested and weren't suspicious when I walked past the open crates with the sticks of dynamite.

So now I have three sticks of dynamite, and all I have to do to make the fuse is soak a woollen thread in lighter fluid. I have everything I need.

I'm going to blow up Bismarck. It all started with him. You think it was good, but it was wrong. Perhaps people will think about it if he's blown up. But perhaps no one will pay any attention if all that's left of him is a heap of debris and rubble. Just as no one notices the decoration in the mountain stream or the chord in the mountains and the pattern in the sand. Things don't have to be noticed in order to be beautiful and true. Nor do deeds.

Who should I share this with, if not with you? Ferdinand is a good boy, and I'm fond of him, but he's a bit boring. They're all like that. They're always quick to pass moral judgement, on the past and on the present, and although their lives are sheltered and it costs them nothing to be moral, they think they're courageous and give themselves airs. I wanted Ferdinand to do better than you and Eik. But his generation also wants everything too big.

You didn't think I had it in me to steal dynamite and blow up monuments? You think what I'm doing is mad? You're happy that I'm doing something mad and that you're no longer alone? I don't yet know when I'll do it. But ever since I've known that I will do it, I feel good.

And I am close to you.

Your Olga

I sat with the letter in my hand and pictured her in my mind's eye: her figure, upright even in old age, slowly making its way through the lamplit streets under the dark sky, the handbag with dynamite, fuse and matches on her arm. I pictured her tampering with the monument. I sensed the silence around her and heard her talking to herself, her restrained humming. I heard the explosion.

I was proud of her. What a great thing when the life someone lives and the act of madness they commit harmonize like melody and counterpoint! And when the two don't just fit together, but are put together by the person herself!

The melody of Olga's life was her love for Herbert and her resistance to him, as fulfilment and as disappointment. After her resistance to Herbert's madness, the mad gesture; a loud bang at the end of a silent life. She set the counterpoint to the melody of her life.

I won't pretend I wasn't hurt, at first, by Olga's last letter. I was boring? But she didn't write that she was bored when she was with me. She wrote of my sheltered life, and I know that my life was sheltered. Perhaps too sheltered, but that's an idle thought.

These are the last lines. They are not a farewell to Olga. I will never bid her farewell. When Adelheid comes, we'll drive to my home town and go to the Bergfriedhof to visit Olga's grave. Of course, I now know that the granddaughter reminded me of the grandmother. How wonderful that I can see Olga's face in Adelheid's!